From the Heart

Sandy Cove Series Book Five

Rosemary Hines

Formatting by 40 Day Publishing

www.40daypublishing.com

Cover photography by Benjamin Hines & and Natalie Knudsen

www.benjaminhines.com

Printed in the United States of America

To Randy

My husband and traveling partner
on this journey of life

To everything there is a season,
A time for every purpose under heaven.

Ecclesiastes 3:3

CHAPTER ONE

She'd first noticed him at the high school baseball game while she watched her older brother in his position as first baseman.

The tall, lanky pitcher with the cockeyed smile and razor-sharp aim took no hostages as he struck out one player after another. His moves drew her focus like a magnet. Even when he pulled off his cap with his right hand and used the same forearm to wipe his brow, there was something manly and attractive that captivated her attention.

She was only sixteen and had never been in love. Shy and awkward around boys, she spent most of her time studying or daydreaming with her girlfriends. When her big brother, Hal, brought his buddies home, she tried to stay out of their way; afraid she'd say or do something that would embarrass him, not to mention herself.

But this time, she got up the courage to ask Hal about his teammate. "So who is that pitcher?" she inquired after the game.

"Who, Phil? He's new this year. Just moved here from Missouri." Hal replied nonchalantly. Then looking at her with a glint in his eye, he added, "Why do you ask?"

"No reason," she answered hastily. "I just don't remember you having him over to the house."

"Should I?" he teased.

"What?"

"Should I 'have him over' for you?" he replied with a wink.

Joan could feel the heat as her face blushed a bright red. Looking away, she mumbled, "Do whatever you want. It's nothing to me."

But when Phil Walker showed up that Sunday afternoon with several other guys from the team, she found herself quaking inside with nerves. Hal made a point of introducing them, and when Phil gave her his crooked smile, using his soft green eyes to lock on hers, her heart raced so fast she thought the whole room could hear.

"So nice to meet you," she managed to say before disappearing into her room. Sitting on the edge of her bed and thinking about his smile, she tried to compose herself, as the sound of the boys' talking and laughter drifted in under her door.

From that day on, she was equally excited and distressed whenever Hal invited Phil over to their house. She analyzed every move she made and any spoken words that passed between them, always trying to wear her cutest clothes and carefully style her hair when she knew he was coming.

Their encounters were brief. A 'hello' as they passed in the kitchen or hallway. Sometimes a quick 'how are you?' or 'good game' would be added to the exchange.

But Joan was in love. With a boy who could have any girl in their school. And she knew her chances were slim to none.

Then it all changed.

The following November, she spotted him across the gymnasium at the homecoming dance. And just as she looked his way, he spotted her, too. His smile got her heart pumping again, and it only got worse when he headed her direction.

"May I have this dance?" he asked after they said their hellos.

Her friend, Ellie, nudged her and tipped her head toward the dance floor. "Go on. I'm off to look for Viv."

After Joan nodded to Phil, he reached out his hand to lead her into the crowd of dancing teens. His grip was warm and strong. And at that moment, Joan suddenly knew that her purpose in life was inextricably linked to his.

They ended up dancing most of the evening. She learned all about his family, his passion for baseball, and his even greater passion for God. He spoke of his grandfather, the pastor of their church in Missouri, and how he'd inspired Phil's own desire to some day lead a congregation.

At the end of the dance, he asked if he could see her again. Her heart now singing in her chest, she tried not to seem too eager as she said yes.

And so began a lifelong journey of joys and heartaches with the only man she'd ever love. Married right out of high school, they struggled to make ends meet as she worked at the local diner to put him through seminary, shelving her own dream of becoming a teacher in order to allow him the opportunity to respond to God's call.

Then came the indescribable joy of becoming parents to a beautiful baby girl. Sheila seemed to make their home complete in spite of its sparse provisions and their continuing financial challenges.

A pastorship that included a parsonage opened the door for this new family to have a home and a mission together as they ministered to a small flock of believers. Joan used her teaching interests and gifts to instruct the little ones during Sunday school and even stretched to lead the women's Bible studies.

Over time, their flock grew. And it seemed their family would as well.

Then tragedy struck when their next child, a boy, was delivered stillborn. As Joan cradled his tiny lifeless body to her chest, she wondered if she'd ever really be able to breathe again herself.

But over time, God brought a healing balm to their brokenness and used this heartache to grow their compassion and ability to minister to others suffering loss. Yes, every step of the way, Joan could see her purpose intertwined with Phil's. They lived and breathed as one, sharing life's unexpected delights and sorrows, and trusting God through it all.

Glancing down at the album in her lap, the one that had taken her on this journey down memory lane, Joan found herself sitting on the bed in her daughter's guest room. Inside still beat the heart of that sixteen-year-old girl who fell in love. But when she glanced up at the mirror over the dresser, she saw an eighty-six year old woman looking back at her.

And her heart that had knitted itself so completely to Phil's was aching with emptiness. Just as she and her beloved husband had laid their tiny son's body in the ground, she'd recently had to place the love of her life there as well. The cancer that devoured his body had claimed her joy and purpose, too.

CHAPTER TWO

Joan gazed at her packed suitcase perched on the edge of the bed. Clothes neatly folded and ready for the trip home.

Home.

What would that mean now without her beloved Phil by her side?

Sinking onto the bed, she rested her hand on the suitcase and sighed. The last couple of weeks had passed so quickly. Phil's final days of releasing his hold on life, the memorial service for neighbors and friends in Mariposa, and then a family service here in Sandy Cove. Days filled to overflowing with no time to think.

Now she'd be alone. Alone with her memories.

Of course, her daughter Sheila had invited her to stay in Sandy Cove indefinitely. "The guest room is yours, Mom," she'd said. But Sheila had her own life to live now. Recently widowed herself, she'd found a second chance at love. And Joan was not going to get in the way.

No. It was time to go home.

Standing, she faced the suitcase again. She zipped it closed and left the solitude of the guest bedroom for one final visit with her daughter before her trip to the airport.

As she ventured into the kitchen, she found Sheila rinsing their breakfast dishes. "I'm all packed, dear," Joan said.

Sheila looked over her shoulder, hands still immersed in the sink. "Okay, Mom. We don't have to leave for another hour. I'll just finish up here, and we can take a little coffee break and discuss your plans."

Joan guessed her daughter would probably make one last effort to convince her to move. *That may be in the future. But for now I need to be at home.*

Sheila grabbed a towel and dried her hands then poured them both a cup of coffee. As they sat down at the kitchen table, Joan took a good look at her only child. Sheila's face was aglow with such a sweet vitality and her eyes sparkled. Love—what a powerful force at any age.

"You look so beautiful, sweetheart."

Her daughter raised her eyebrows and smiled. "Thanks, Mom. What brought that on?"

"I just noticed how youthful and alive you are looking these days. I'll bet it has a lot to do with that professor of yours," she added, winking.

Sheila cleared her throat and looked away as if embarrassed.

"It suits you," Joan continued.

"What?"

"Love. You wear it well."

"Okay, first of all, no one said anything about love. Rick and I are taking it slow," she replied.

Joan smiled. "Whatever you say, dear." She stirred some cream into her coffee and sat back against the chair.

"So have you given any more thought to moving in with me?" Sheila asked. "We'd all really love to have you here, Mom, and Caleb is so in love with Thumper that he'd get plenty of attention and playtime."

Joan thought about Thumper and how he would adjust to life back in Mariposa without his master. Phil and that dog had been inseparable ever since she and her husband had picked him out of a litter of playful golden retrievers. She'd hoped for a sweet girl pup, but Thumper had chosen

12

Phil, laying across his feet and looking up with those doleful eyes. Yes, Caleb was a good diversion for old Thumper. "I'm keeping your offer in mind, Sheila. But right now, there's a tug on my heart to get home."

Her daughter nodded. "Okay. Well, I'll keep after you. Expect a lot of phone calls from here," she warned.

"I'll look forward to each and every one of them."

They sat quietly for a few moments, and Joan breathed a silent prayer of thanksgiving that their family was so close and always welcomed them back with open arms. Then, out of the blue, a wave of grief washed over her. It wouldn't be 'them' any more. *Oh, Phil. How am I going to do this life now?*

"Are you okay, Mom?" Sheila asked, concern furrowing her brow.

Joan rallied herself and forced a smile. "Fine. I'm fine, honey." She pushed against the table as she stood. "Everything's arranged with the dog, right?"

"Yep. Steve will be bringing him when he comes to pick you up, and the airlines have been notified. It's all set." Sheila paused and then added, "Have you talked to your pastor this morning?"

"Yes. Lawrence is set to pick us up at the airport. I gave him the flight number, and he's bringing the church van so Thumper's crate won't be a problem."

Just then the doorbell rang. "Must be Steve," Sheila said, taking their cups and placing them on the counter before going to answer it. Joan followed her out to greet her granddaughter's husband. As soon as the door opened, Thumper raced inside, wagging his tail in greeting. Taking one quick sniff at each of them, he headed back into the house.

"Thumper, get back here," Steve called. "I wonder why he took off like that?"

"He's probably looking for Dad," Sheila said. "Come here, boy," she called, and he reappeared momentarily from the hallway then disappeared into the kitchen.

"I'll get your bags, Joan," Steve offered, heading for the guest room with Joan on his tail.

She supervised his retrieval of her luggage, and then the doorbell rang again. "Who could that be?" she asked.

"I think I have an idea," Steve replied knowingly. As he rolled the suitcases out to the front door, in walked Michelle and the kids.

"I know we said goodbye last night," she began. "But as soon as Steve pulled out of the driveway, the kids and I decided to come over and see you one more time."

Joan smiled and nodded. "Come here, you two!"

Madison and Caleb walked into her open arms.

"Can't you just stay here with us?" Caleb asked.

"Yeah. Grandma. We want you here in Sandy Cove," Madison agreed.

Joan gave them both a squeeze then opened her arms and took a step back to take in their sweet faces. "I promise I'll come back soon," she said. "But there are some things I need to attend to at home."

Michelle took her turn for a hug. Whispering in her grandmother's ear, she said, "Call us anytime. We will come get you and bring you back."

"Thanks, sweetheart. You don't know what a comfort that is," Joan murmured softly in her granddaughter's ear. Then releasing her, she turned to Steve. We'd better round up that dog and get going so I don't miss my flight."

They found Thumper in the kitchen, curled up by the back door.

"Can I take him out one last time before you leave?" Caleb asked.

"Two minutes," his father replied. "And then we've got to go."

14

As Thumper followed Caleb outside, Steve took the luggage to the car to load it.

Tearful goodbyes followed as they got themselves and the dog into the van, and Joan waved to her daughter, granddaughter, and great grandchildren. She watched Caleb bury his face in his mother's side.

"He's really going to miss you," Steve said. "We all are."

She nodded, afraid to test her voice in reply.

As Joan navigated through airport security and onto the plane, she realized this was her first time to fly alone. Gripping her boarding pass in her hand, she smiled courageously at each passenger who looked up at her as she made her way down the aisle in search of her seat. Steve had assured her that she had an aisle seat. Easier to get in and out, he'd said. But when she got to her row, someone else was sitting in the seat assigned to her. A rather large man with long legs spilling out into the walkway. The seat beside him was empty, and in the window seat, a young man, who appeared to be in his early twenties, was listening to earphones as he looked out over the tarmac.

"Excuse me," Joan said politely.

The man looked up and stood, gesturing to the middle seat.

Joan hesitated a moment before deciding to take it. After all, the man was very tall, and he'd be cramped in that middle seat.

As the plane ascended, she glanced over at the young man on her other side and noticed a Bible on his lap. When he removed his earphones, she commented, "I see you have a Bible there."

"Yeah. I was just listening to a message by one of my favorite pastors," he replied. "You read the Bible much?"

She smiled. "As a matter of fact, I do. My husband was a pastor."

"Really? Cool," he replied. "I'm about to begin Bible college myself. Hoping to be a youth pastor someday."

His youthful enthusiasm reminded her of Phil when they were courting. And his sweet smile was a ringer for her husband's. *I wonder where the years will take this fellow,* she thought as she replayed Phil's life of service.

"So tell me about your husband," the young man said. "Where was he a pastor?"

And just like that, God provided a travel companion for Joan's journey home. Between her stories of Phil and his ministries, as well as this boy's dreams of service, the time flew by. When the aircraft wheels touched down, her new friend turned to her and said, "I'm really glad we got to talk. Your husband sounds like a great guy. Thanks for telling me about him."

"Thank you for listening," she replied with a smile. "I'm sure God has a special plan for you, young man."

✎

Pastor Lawrence Taylor was waiting at the luggage claim area when Joan arrived. After they exchanged hugs and greetings, she turned to introduce the young man she'd met to her pastor, but he was gone.

They retrieved her bags and went through the process of getting Thumper and his crate. Then they were on the road, headed back to the Walkers' home. Forcing herself to stay awake for the drive, Joan was exhausted by the time they pulled into the long driveway. Thumper eagerly bolted out of the back of the van and ran around the property.

"For an old dog, he sure has a lot of energy," Lawrence observed.

Joan nodded. "I hope he'll do alright without Phil. He was so used to their walks together every day," she added.

"Maybe your neighbor boy will offer to take him sometimes."

"Yeah. Trent's such a nice kid. I'm sure he'll help."

"Well, let's get your luggage inside," he said, lifting the suitcases to the ground and rolling them toward the house.

After all of Joan's things were in her room and her suitcases were on her bed for ease of unpacking, he started for the car again. "I've got one more thing to bring in."

He returned with a small cooler. Placing it on the counter, he began lifting out the contents. "Catherine made you a casserole for dinner. It's one of Matt's and my favorites. She said to tell you to heat it at three-fifty for forty-five minutes. And she included some of her homemade biscuits and a slice of apple pie," he added with a smile as he held up each container before placing them into the refrigerator.

"Your wife is such a sweetheart," Joan said. "Please tell her thank you. As you can guess, the cupboards are pretty bare here."

"About that," he began. "She also said to tell you she'd be here in the morning to take you to the market. She sent along these zucchini muffins for breakfast," he said as he pulled a bag out of the cooler. "She said you'd asked for the recipe one time, so she figured you liked them."

"I do, indeed," Joan replied, feeling overwhelmed by the thoughtfulness of her pastor and his wife.

"Just give Catherine a call in the morning when you're up, and you two can set up a time to go to the store together."

"Thank you again, so much. I really do appreciate all of this." Joan held out her arms and gave Lawrence a warm hug. "Can I get you a cup of coffee or tea?"

"No thanks. I'd better get going. I've still got a couple of appointments this afternoon, and I promised to drop by the hospital on my way home."

Joan nodded. "I know how busy the life of a pastor can be. You scoot along, and I'll get settled back into my home here."

"Call me if you need anything." He looked her squarely in the eye. "I mean it, Joan. Anytime. Day or night."

She smiled. "Thanks. I'll be fine. But I promise I'll call if I need you."

As soon as he was gone, she sank into her kitchen chair and called Sheila to let her know she'd arrived home safely. Then she sat for a few minutes, the exhaustion of the trip taking its toll.

Gazing around the empty room, she sighed. "I can do this," she said aloud as if to convince herself. "I'll just unpack my bags, and then have a cup of tea on the front porch before I fix my dinner." But standing up required more energy than she could muster. It was Thumper's scratch at the door that finally pulled her to her feet. "I'm coming, big boy," she called out as she headed in his direction.

As soon as the door was open, he stormed through the house, scouring every corner before returning with Phil's slippers in his mouth. Joan looked down at his eager eyes and could barely contain her sorrow. "I'm so sorry, boy. He's not here." She reached down and stroked his head, his big brown eyes starring up at her quizzically.

"Let's get you a little treat," she said, heading for the pantry. Retrieving a box of dog biscuits, she held one out to him, coaxing the slippers out of his mouth in exchange.

While he chomped on the biscuit, she took her husband's slippers and put them back in the closet. As she gently stroked Phil's shirts, a subtle fragrance wafted from them. She buried her nose in one of the sleeves and breathed in the remaining scent of English Leather. It was a gift she gave him each Christmas. A tradition since their first year as husband and wife.

Closing her eyes, she could hear his voice in the recesses of her mind. "I love you, Jo." And then his final words as he'd stared up to heaven before leaving earth. "I see it. I see it all." Oh how she wished she were there with him now, gazing into the face of God.

Turning to leave the closet, she carefully closed the door behind her, knowing that Thumper would try at least one more time to retrieve his slippers. Engrained in him since he was a pup, it was part of their nightly ritual. Then she returned to the kitchen and gave him his dinner.

Although she forced herself to heat the casserole from Catherine Taylor, she could only stomach a few bites of food before the solitude began to strangle her. She picked up the phone to dial Sheila's number again then stopped and hung up. "I can't keep disturbing her. Besides, I've got to unpack and make a grocery list for the morning," she said aloud. Thumper looked over, watching her to see if she was talking to him.

Reaching down, she ruffled his fur. "Come on. You can keep me company," she said, as she headed to the bedroom with him on her heels. After unpacking her bags, she glanced at the clock on the nightstand. Only 7:30. But she felt so tired.

"Shall we call it a night, Thumper?"

As if he understood her perfectly, he walked over to Phil's side, curled up in a ball on his doggie bed, and went to sleep.

Joan changed into her nightgown, brushed her teeth, and was about to slip into bed when she remembered that Thumper would need one more trip outside. Phil was always the one to take him out before bed, and while she'd been in Sandy Cove staying with Sheila, Thumper had been in the care of her granddaughter, Michelle, and her family.

Wrapping her robe around her and tying its belt, she roused the dog from his bed and took him out back to do his business. As she reached for the knob to let him out, she realized she'd left it unlocked earlier. *I've got to remember these things.* Once again she was painfully aware of how much her beloved husband had taken care of for her.

"I'm trying, Phil," she said to the air.

As soon as Thumper returned, the two of them headed for bed. Joan reached for her husband's pillow and hugged it to her chest as she drifted off to sleep.

CHAPTER THREE

When she awoke the next morning, Joan was in the same position she'd fallen asleep in the night before. She could hear a whimpering sound in the distance. The first words out of her mouth, before she even opened her eyes were, "Phil, the dog needs to go out."

And then she remembered. Thumper was her responsibility now. Grabbing her robe off the foot of the bed and stepping into her slippers, she went to let the dog out. As she stood on the porch, she noticed the flowerbeds were looking a little ragged. Time for some weeding and fertilizer. She'd try to get to that after breakfast.

But first, she needed some time with the Lord.

Feeding Thumper and then making herself a cup of tea, she sat in her rocking chair and reached for a Bible in the basket at her feet. Flipping it open, she began reading the book of Psalms. Words of pain, fear, and anguish were combined with precious promises and praises to the God who would never leave nor forsake her.

The more she read, the more her heart found peace. There was something about the record of others' struggles and triumphs that fanned a flame of hope within.

Her stomach rumbled, reminding her she'd barely eaten the night before. The zucchini muffins Catherine had sent called to her from the kitchen. As sun filtered in through the kitchen window, she sat in its early morning warmth, enjoyed her treat, and began drafting a grocery list.

A soft knock on the front door caught her attention. She padded out to the front room and pulled aside the lace curtain of the window to peer outside.

The neighbor boy, Trent, was walking down the porch steps. She quickly opened the door and immediately spotted the box of mail at her feet. "Trent?" she called out.

He turned and looked her way, raising his hand in a friendly wave. "Hello, Mrs. Walker. Hope I didn't wake you up."

"No. I've been up for over an hour. Thanks for bringing my mail over," she added with a smile.

"You're welcome. We saw your lights on last night, so we figured you were home."

"Would you like to come inside?" she asked. "I've got an extra zucchini muffin waiting for a taker."

"No thanks. I've got to get to school. Football practice," he replied. "Coach is pretty strict about us being on time."

"Has that started already? I guess I've lost track a little."

"Yeah. Summer's basically over for me. We have practice this week and next. Then the week after that, classes start again."

It was moving into fall. Joan's favorite time of year. But this fall would be different than all the rest. This time she'd be facing it alone.

"Can I carry that box in for you?" Trent asked.

She gave it a little nudge with her foot to test its weight. It didn't budge. "That would be wonderful. But I don't want to make you late."

"No problem. Where would you like it?"

"On the dining room table would be good," she replied, holding open the door for him.

Setting it down at the head of the table, he said, "Well, I'd better get going."

"You take care at practice, dear. And be sure to drink plenty of water in this heat," she added.

"Yes, Ma'am." He walked out the door, took the porch steps two at a time, and started down the walkway. Then he stopped, turned around, and added, "I'm really sorry about Mr. Walker. He was a cool guy."

She nodded and gave him her best smile. "Thanks, Trent. He thought you were pretty cool yourself."

After he'd disappeared around the bend at the end of their driveway, she headed back inside to begin the task of sorting through the mail. She'd just finished pulling out and tossing all the junk mail, when the phone rang. It was Sheila.

"Hi, Mom," her daughter's voice greeted her. "How was your first night home?"

They chatted for several minutes and then Joan asked about Rick.

Sheila's voice picked up tempo as she talked about the man who was clearly winning her heart. "I honestly can't believe this is happening to me at my age," she said.

"Oh, you're not so old, dear," Joan replied. "You two still have a lot of good years left. Why, your father and I enjoyed the last twenty-five years just as much as our first," she added, some of her recent treasured memories drifting through her mind.

"Thanks, Mom. That's a good reminder for me." She paused and then confessed, "I think I love him. I mean really love him, Mom."

Joan could hear the excitement and joy in her daughter's voice. She sat back and smiled. And in her mind, she could once again hear Phil's voice, "I love you, Jo."

"Mom? Are you still there?"

"Yes. Sorry, honey. Just some old memories distracting me," she explained. "But enough of that. I'm really happy for you two. I assume he feels the same, right?"

"He says he does. We're getting pretty serious in our talks about the future."

"Well good, sweetheart. I hope this works out for you." Joan meant it with all her heart. Nothing would please her more than to have her daughter happily married again.

They chatted for a few minutes, and then Joan remembered her pastor's wife's offer to take her shopping for groceries. "I've got to get going, dear," she said. "Catherine Taylor is taking me to the market this morning, and I need to give her a call to set up a time."

As soon as they'd hung up, she pulled out her phone book, flipped to the back, and found Lawrence and Catherine's home number.

By the time Catherine dropped her off from their trip to the market, Joan was hungry for lunch. After unpacking the groceries, she made herself a quick sandwich, and Thumper planted himself at her feet, gazing up with hopeful eyes.

"What are *you* looking at?" she asked, with raised eyebrows.

He just kept staring.

"I have no intention of sneaking you bites from the table the way your papa used to."

As if he understood, he sighed, sunk to the floor, and rested his head on his front paws, defeat written across his face.

"Oh, all right," Joan said. She broke off a corner of the sandwich and handed it to him. He was immediately on his feet, carefully retrieving the morsel and wagging his tail in gratitude. "Now go lie down," she commanded, watching him head for his usual spot by the back door.

"Phil Walker, you spoiled that dog, and now I'm stuck with the consequences." She shook her head and turned her attention back to her meal.

After lunch, she had the rest of the mail to sort through, bills to pay, and weeds to pull. Her chores kept her busy until nightfall.

Then the loneliness returned, sneaking through the door when she wasn't looking. There was something about eating dinner alone that killed her appetite. Phil had often been gone during the day, so she was accustomed to eating breakfast and lunch on her own. But dinner—that was their special time to reconnect, share each other's day, and lift up their family and friends in prayer.

Even Thumper's focused attention did nothing to alleviate the hollowness in her heart. And his repeat performance with Phil's slippers reminded her that she was going to have to attend to sorting through and giving away her precious husband's personal items.

She stared at her spaghetti dinner, one of their favorite meals, and pushed it away. *Maybe I'll reheat it tomorrow*, she thought with a sigh. Wandering into the living room, she settled herself in front of the television and turned on the news. Seemed that the world was falling apart, too. Wars, natural disasters, and political scandals consumed most of the current events reported.

Lord, help us, she prayed, as she flipped the channels until she found an old comedy to fill her empty evening.

CHAPTER FOUR

As the next couple of weeks slipped by, Joan found herself with more and more time on her hands. She'd finally figured out the bills and gotten them caught up, at least she was pretty sure she had. The weeds in the flowerbeds had been conquered through a combination of her efforts—perched on a stepstool—and hiring Trent over the weekends to help out. And she'd gotten all her clothes from the trip washed, pressed, and put away.

There was one job she just couldn't seem to bring herself to do—cleaning out Phil's side of the closet. Having his slacks and shirts hanging in place, his shoes neatly lined up under them, and his slippers resting in their spot was somehow comforting to her. It was as if he'd gone away on a trip and would be returning to resume their life together.

Oh, she'd tried a few times. But she'd end up standing there staring at his clothes, leaning into them, and searching for his scent. Then she'd find some excuse to put it off for another day or two. *I'll get around to it*, she reassured herself. But the time never seemed right.

Then one day an unexpected rain swept through Mariposa, and her plans to accompany Catherine on some errands and then work in the garden were cancelled. She had nothing to do.

"I refuse to get caught up in daytime TV," she announced to Thumper, whose tail twitched slightly in response. "Come on, fella. Let's get this over with."

Thumper rose to his feet and followed her into the bedroom, the sound of the rain pounding loudly on the roof.

She began carrying her husband's shirts and their hangers from the closet and placing them on the bed. Thumper must have smelled Phil on the clothes because he began circling the bed, his nose lifted as he whimpered excitedly.

"Settle down, boy," Joan coaxed, taking a moment to stroke his back.

But he wouldn't listen. He continued to pace and whine, until finally she decided to send him out of the room and close the door. "Sometimes I think this is as hard on him as it is on me," she muttered under her breath.

Opening one of the windows, she breathed in the fragrance of the rain. "Thank you, Lord. We really need this," she prayed aloud. Her lawn had developed brown patches, in spite of the sprinklers, and the nearby hills were parched.

Turning her attention back to the shirts on the bed, she began carefully removing them from their hangers, handling each one lovingly as she tri-folded them as if to create a department store display.

A faded barbecue sauce stain on one reminded her of a church picnic and the way Phil had playfully romped with a few of the kids from the neighborhood. A crisp white button-down collared shirt was his "wedding and funeral" best. Even into his eighties, he looked so handsome wearing it with his navy blue tie and gray suit.

Each shirt brought back memories. Their fiftieth anniversary, baby dedications of grandchildren and great grandchildren, his favorite to wear when he preached a message at the senior home, and his old flannels for puttering around in the garden or garage.

She studied the neatly folded stack. "I wonder if Steve would want any of these?" she asked herself, thinking about her granddaughter's husband, the attorney. She picked up the phone and called Michelle. But a voicemail recording answered. Joan hated to talk to machines, so she hung up. *I'll try again later.*

The slacks were easier, although she did find some lists and notes in a few of the pockets. Seeing Phil's handwriting on scraps of paper, even if they were just grocery lists or a Bible verse he was memorizing—they stopped her in her tracks. She ran her fingers over his writing, and then carefully placed them on the dresser.

"I'm turning into an old fool, saving Phil's pocket scraps like this," she said.

Thumper whimpered and scratched on the door, but when she opened it to let him back in, he bolted down the stairs. *Must need to go outside.*

Sure enough, he was standing by the door, his nose pressed to the jamb. She peered out at the pouring rain. "How badly do you need to go out?" she asked.

He scratched the door and whimpered again.

"Okay, okay. Make it quick." She opened the door, and he flew out, immediately running to his favorite tree to relieve himself. "I'd better get some towels," she said, heading for the laundry room. Phil kept a stack of old ones in there for just such a purpose. She found them on the far corner of the counter, grabbed a couple, and went back into the kitchen to spread one on the floor and have the other ready to dry the dog off as much as she could.

Thumper was a water dog, and he came bounding back inside fully energized by his run in the rain. Before she could get the towel on him, he shook himself vigorously, spraying Joan and the room. "Oh my word! Settle down, now. You hear?"

She tried to wrestle the towel over him, but he took off running through the house and rolling on the living room floor. By the time she got in there, he'd left a wet and muddy mess on the tan carpet.

"Thumper! Bad dog!" she exclaimed. Sinking down on the couch, the towel still clutched in her hands, she started to cry. Phil always knew how to handle their dog. And, as much as she loved the beast, he'd never responded to her authority with the same respect as he did to Phil's.

She wept for several minutes, her sniffling attempts to steady herself blending with the steady sound of the rain. Suddenly she felt very old and tired. The energy she'd rallied to pack up Phil's clothes vanished and the very thought of trying to clean the carpet—well, it was more than she could fathom.

Stretching out on the couch, she rested her head on a throw pillow and continued to clutch the unused towel to her chest. Soon she drifted off to sleep.

And then she was in the kitchen, making one of her famous lemon meringue pies. The screen door slapped against the jamb. "I'm home, dear," Phil's familiar voice called out.

"In here," she called back.

He came and stood beside her, dipping his finger into the gooey lemon mixture.

"Philip Walker, get your hands out of the pie filling," she scolded. Turning to look him in the eye, she saw a playful smile light up his face.

"I love you, Jo," he replied with a wink, sticking his lemony finger into his mouth and murmuring his appreciation of its sweet flavor.

The phone rang and she turned to answer it, but it wasn't on the counter in its usual place. "Where's the phone?" she asked.

But no one answered.

The ringing continued, and she spun to face Phil. He was gone.

"Phil?" she called out over the persistent ringing.

30

Something cold pressed against her face. Opening her eyes, she saw Thumper staring at her, just inches away. Struggling to sit up on the couch, she realized she'd fallen asleep. Another ring of the phone let her know the call was real. She reached for the phone on the end table.

"Hello?"

"Grandma? Are you okay? I noticed you'd called earlier, so I thought I'd better call back. The phone's been ringing for a long time."

"Sorry dear, but I fell asleep."

"Oh, no. I didn't mean to wake you. I almost hung up after half a dozen rings, but then I started getting worried. Are you home alone?"

Joan flashed back to her dream about Phil. It had been so real. She wanted nothing more than to resume it.

"Grandma?"

"Oh. Yeah. I was just thinking about a dream I had while I was asleep. Your grandfather was with me in the kitchen, and I was baking a lemon pie."

After a pause, her granddaughter said, "You must be missing him terribly."

Joan nodded her head and sighed. "It's a little rough. But don't you go worrying about me, sweetheart. Thumper's here to keep me company, and I've been pretty busy getting things accomplished around here. Speaking of which, I've been cleaning out Grandpa's side of the closet, and I was wondering if Steve could use any of his shirts or jackets."

"It's sweet of you to think of him, Grandma, but his closet is pretty full already with button down shirts for work. Pick a couple of your favorites, and I'm sure he'd love to have them. Maybe you could think about donating the rest to the Alzheimer's Home where he ministered. Some of the residents might appreciate them, or they could sell them in their thrift store."

"Good idea. Okay, I'll save a few for Steve and donate the rest." She tried to sound cheerful and upbeat, but her brain was feeling a little fuzzy from her nap, and her heart was wishing she were back in the kitchen with Phil. *Snap out of it. Time to focus on your granddaughter,* she silently chided herself. "How are things with you and your family?" she asked.

"We're all doing fine. Getting back in the swing of school. We started classes on Monday. The kids are excited to be with their friends again, and I'm trying to learn 180 new names of students in my English classes."

"That must be quite a chore, Michelle," Joan replied. "Your grandfather was so proud of all you do at that middle school. Me, too."

"Thanks, Grandma."

"Well, say hi to Madison and Caleb for me. And thanks for calling."

After they'd hung up, Joan examined the muddy spot on the carpet. *Better get to this,* she thought as she forced her tired body to a standing position. A clap of thunder reminded her of the slapping sound of the screen door in her dream. Heading for the laundry room, she began searching for the spot cleaner for the carpet.

Scrubbing the chemicals into the rug brought a spasm to her lower back. It was difficult for her to right herself and stand up again. She carefully shuffled back to the laundry room, replaced the bottle of cleaning solution, and then made her way to the kitchen to see if she could find something simple for dinner.

Pulling a can of soup out of the pantry, she emptied its contents into a pan. Then placing it on the burner to heat, she tried to figure out how she'd feed the dog without bending over. Her back was so tight, and sharp pain shot through it if she moved the wrong way.

The box of dog biscuits was at eye level, and she decided Thumper would have to make do with them for his dinner. She dropped several on the floor and the big dog gobbled them up instantly then looked back at her for more. "Okay, big boy. Just a few more and then that's it for tonight." She took another handful from the box and let them fall to the floor at her feet.

A bubbly sound caught her attention just in time to see her soup boiling over and spilling onto the stovetop. Although the bottom of the soup was burned, she was able to salvage enough to fill a bowl. Adding a few saltine crackers to her meal, she eased herself into a chair and gradually consumed her dinner, while her back continued to tighten.

By the time she was finished eating, she wasn't sure she'd be able to stand up. Bracing herself by placing her hands on the table, she slowly eased her way out of the chair. She knew she needed help, but whom could she call?

Then her pastor's words came back to her. "Call me anytime. I mean it, Joan. Day or night." As the wife of a pastor herself, she knew the many calls that came in at all hours, and the countless nights Phil had found himself assisting one of the church members in distress. Sometimes he'd even taken her along, especially if the caller were a woman.

Joan knew Lawrence and Catherine had multiple demands on their time. And she hated to call them out on a wet night like this. But she couldn't think of anyone else to call except Trent or his parents, and she hated to bother them after all they'd done to help her since Phil's illness.

She shuffled over to the phone and dialed the Taylor's number. Catherine picked up on the second ring. "Joan, is that you?" she asked.

"Yes. I'm so sorry to bother you, but I've hurt my back."

"We'll be right over," Catherine replied. Joan could hear her explaining the situation to Lawrence. "Now you just stay put, Joan. Don't try to move around. We can be there in fifteen minutes."

CHAPTER FIVE

Joan stood leaning against the counter. Even a walk back to the table seemed a challenge, and making it to the couch was out of the question. Thankfully, she'd left the door unlocked after letting Thumper back in. She was still standing there staring out the window when Lawrence's car pulled into the driveway.

They spotted her in the window, and she gestured to the back door. The rain had stopped, but the driveway was slick, and she could see Catherine carefully navigating around several puddles. Soon they were by her side, and Lawrence took her by the elbow to help her gradually make her way to the couch.

"I've brought an ice pack," Catherine said. "Larry will help you lay down on it. After we ice it for about fifteen minutes, we'll see how you're doing. We can take you to the E.R. if it doesn't feel better."

Joan nodded, happy to have someone else take charge. An ice pack sounded a little strange to her. Seemed her mother always brought out the hot water bottle for any muscle aches, so that's what she and Phil usually used. But Catherine explained that it would help with the inflammation and that heat was for later, after the first twenty-four hours.

Once they'd gotten her stretched out on the couch, Catherine grabbed a blanket and placed it over her. "This will help the rest of you keep warm," she explained with a caring smile.

"Thank you both so much," Joan said, tears beginning to fill her eyes.

"We're happy to help," Lawrence replied. "Now that we've got you on ice, let's pray."

Joan nodded. She loved the sound of his words. It reminded her so much of her sweet Phil. She soaked in the blessing of the prayer and began to feel the tight grip of loneliness loosening from her heart.

Other than Lawrence carrying her luggage to the bedroom when he brought her home from the airport, Catherine helping her in with groceries, and Trent's quick entrance to place her mail on the table, there hadn't been another human being in the house but her for the past three weeks. If it weren't for Sunday's worship services and occasional errands, she'd be living a very solitary existence.

Even at church, standing amongst her friends, she often felt alone without Phil by her side. Was this how life was supposed to end? She didn't want to be a burden to anyone, and all of her alternatives seemed to point in that direction.

After fifteen minutes, Lawrence helped her swing her feet to the floor and sit up. Her back felt a little better, but she still needed to be very careful how she moved. "Have you eaten anything tonight?" Catherine asked.

"A little soup and some crackers."

"Let's get something more substantial into your stomach, and then I'd suggest you take some aspirin. Are you okay to take aspirin?"

"Yes. I take it for my arthritis."

"Okay. I'll go wrestle something up in the kitchen, and after you eat we'll get the aspirin." She disappeared into the kitchen, and then poked her head back out. "Your dog is crying at the door. Should I let him out?"

"That would be great, Catherine. Thank you," Joan replied, trying to push herself to a standing position.

"What are you doing?" Lawrence asked.

"I've got to take a towel into the kitchen for Thumper. He'll be a muddy mess when he comes back in."

"You let me handle that," he replied. "Where are the towels?"

She pointed to the one she'd gotten out to use before. It was resting on the arm of a nearby chair.

"Okay. Now you just sit still. Don't try to get up."

She nodded. "When Catherine has a minute, I need to use the ladies' room," she said, feeling like a helpless fool.

"I'll tell her," he replied.

A minute later, Catherine reappeared. "Let's get you to the bathroom," she said, offering Joan her hand. With the help of her friend, Joan was able to stand. They slowly moved in the direction of their destination.

Joan felt so embarrassed to have to ask Catherine to help her with such a personal need, but sitting and standing required assistance. Catherine functioned with ease and compassion. It was clear this was not her first time helping someone navigate a bathroom.

After eating the eggs and toast prepared for her, Joan took a couple of aspirins.

"You can ice it again now for fifteen more minutes. We'll do that a couple of times before you go to bed."

"I think I can manage now," Joan replied, trying to convince herself as much as them.

"If you don't mind, we'll just stay here with you and make sure you are okay," Lawrence said.

They ended up watching an old movie on television, and after icing her back three times, Joan was able to walk on her own. Catherine helped her get ready for bed and then she and Lawrence headed for home, leaving a promise behind that they would check on her in the morning.

As Joan began to fall asleep, she hoped she'd dream about Phil again. But a dreamless night soon became morning, and she awoke to the sound of the phone ringing on the nightstand.

Reaching over carefully, she picked it up. "Hello?"

"Hi, Mom. It's Sheila. Catherine Taylor called me this morning and told me about your back. How are you feeling?"

Joan pushed herself up to a sitting position. Her back was still very stiff, but the pain was manageable. "I'm doing a little better, honey."

"I'm glad they were able to come over and help you out last night. But, Mom, you really need to think about moving up here."

"I know. Believe me, I'm thinking about it," she heard herself saying. "I've been going through your father's things and trying to get things organized here. Then I can figure out what's next."

"So you're seriously considering moving here?" Sheila's voice sounded hopeful. It warmed Joan's heart to feel so wanted and welcome in her daughter's life. Especially now, when Sheila was seriously dating someone.

"I'm taking it under consideration, dear. But I haven't made any decisions yet. Leaving our home will be difficult. There are just so many memories here..." her voice faded off as she thought about how much her surroundings helped her feel close to Phil.

"I know, Mom. I still miss our place in Seal Beach. But there's nothing like being close to family. And the kids would love to have you and Thumper back up here. Caleb asks about 'his' dog all the time."

Joan smiled. In her mind's eye, she could see Caleb's romps with Thumper from her recent stay in Sandy Cove after Phil's death. And it was awfully hard for her to keep up with the dog and his antics. Maybe Sheila was right.

Her daughter's voice interrupted her thoughts. "Michelle said she called yesterday, but you didn't mention anything about your back acting up."

"No, I hurt it after our conversation. I was trying to clean up some mud Thumper trailed in from the backyard."

"Well, take it easy today. Don't try to do anything physical. Promise?"

"I promise, honey."

After they'd hung up, she carefully got up from the bed, slipped out of her nightgown and into a housecoat. "No need to get dressed today," she said to the air. "I guess I'll just relax and write some letters and watch a little TV today."

Thumper stood at the door watching her.

"I'm coming, boy. Hopefully I can bend down to get your food for breakfast."

He wagged his tail and followed her to the kitchen.

By gripping the counter's edge and carefully bending her knees, she managed to scoop some food out of Thumper's bin. Rather than picking up the bowl, she just aimed carefully and poured. Most of it hit the target, and Thumper happily cleaned up the rest.

Catherine dropped by later that morning with a basket of food. A hearty turkey sandwich and salad for lunch, and a thick stew for her dinner. "Now you rest. And keep the phone nearby to call us if you need us," she said.

Joan could imagine the sacrifice this meant to Catherine. With the women's ministry to run, and all the other demands of being a pastor's wife, she knew full well that time was in short supply.

"Thank you so much," she replied, grasping her friend's hand and looking her in the eye. "Please don't worry about me. I'm not alone." She pointed heavenward and gave Catherine her best smile.

The day dragged by as she tried to rest her back. Thumper slept on the floor beside the couch—her constant companion—and she found herself talking to him about the things on her mind. Occasionally he'd lift his head and study her face, then plop back down and drift off to sleep.

Joan prayed a lot that day. But her prayers seemed to fall back to earth before reaching the throne room.

By the following day, she could feel her back loosening its grip on her. She took a gentle walk down to the mailbox at the end of their long driveway and was delighted to find a letter from her great granddaughter, Madison.

Michelle's younger child, Caleb, had begun corresponding with his birthmother, and twelve year old Madison seemed to be looking for a pen pal herself. Apparently Michelle had suggested Joan.

The letter was actually rather lengthy, filled with tales of Maddie's family and friends, with special mention of Luke—a boy her age, who was the son of Michelle and Steve's close friends Ben and Kelly. Ben had actually started a church in Sandy Cove, and Phil was quite impressed with his preaching. It was the church Michelle's family and Sheila now attended.

Joan and her daughter had noticed a special bond developing between Madison and Luke. *Puppy love*, Joan thought.

As she devoured the letter, handwritten on notebook paper, she pictured her loved ones and their busy lives in Sandy Cove. It was so sweet to get a peek at their world through Madison's eyes.

The letter ended with a plea to seriously consider moving. "We all miss you, Grandma! And Caleb talks about Thumper all the time."

Joan smiled. What a gift to know her great grandchildren like this. *Maybe she's right. After all, how much longer do I have?*

CHAPTER SIX

A week later, Joan made her decision. She'd pack up the old house and move to Sandy Cove.

Sheila seemed thrilled with her decision. "I'm coming down, Mom. We can sort through everything together. And I'll get the guest room ready."

As much as she loved the idea of living with her daughter, Joan was determined not to get in the way of Sheila's relationship with Rick. "I've been thinking about that, honey, and I'd like to live on my own somewhere. Where I can still feel like I have a place to call home."

"But, Mom," her daughter began.

"No buts. The best thing you can do for me right now is to look into what's available for me up there. Maybe a senior apartment? Or some kind of assisted living home? I'm not getting any younger here, and I will not be a burden to you or Michelle."

Although Sheila protested, Joan finally convinced her she was serious. "Otherwise, I'm not moving up there," she declared.

"You're certainly being stubborn about this, Mom."

Joan smiled. She knew when she'd won a battle with her daughter. "Yep. I'm a stubborn old coot. Now you get to looking around for a nice place for me up there, and I'll start sorting through all my accumulated stuff. Once I know the size of the place where I'll be living, it will help me know how much I should keep and what to give away."

The following day, she hired Trent to carry boxes down from the attic. "You be careful up there, young man. I'm sure there are plenty of little eight-legged critters who've been making their homes in the nooks and crannies."

"I'm not afraid of spiders, Mrs. Walker. But I'll be careful," he added with a grin.

Two hours later, the living room was full of an assortment of boxes of various sizes. Half of them were handwritten sermons from Phil's days as a full-time pastor. "Well, would you look at that?" she exclaimed. "I had no idea we still had these stored up there."

Trent pulled out one of the files. "He wrote out all these?"

"Yep. Every one of them. He liked to use pencil so he could make corrections." She paged through the files, which were in order from Genesis to Revelation. "I wonder if Ben would want any of these?"

"What?" Trent asked.

"Oh, nothing. Just talking to myself."

"Okay. Well that's the last of the boxes," Trent said, standing off to the side.

Joan reached for her purse and pulled out her wallet. "What do I owe you, son?"

"Nothing. It was no big deal. Let me know if you need anything else moved." He started walking toward the door to leave.

"How about a slice of lemon pie?" Her dream had sparked a craving for it that would not leave her alone.

"Now that I'd take," he replied with a grin, following her into the kitchen.

It took Joan several days to go through the boxes that didn't contain sermons. She'd already determined that if

Ben weren't interested in Phil's messages, she'd keep them and try to compile some kind of devotional notebook for the grandkids and great grandkids.

The rest of the boxes contained memorabilia from their early years of marriage and Sheila's childhood. She pulled out a plaster mold of Sheila's hand from kindergarten. Placing her own hand over the small impression, she marveled to think that even Sheila's grandchildren had bigger hands than this now.

There were paintings that had seen their day on the refrigerator display, prize ribbons for school awards, and even a few book reports that had earned extra high marks. Each treasure brought back a flood of memories.

One shoebox was stuffed with old photos from their vacations. Faded images of Yosemite, the Sequoia National Forest, and Yellowstone were mixed in with various road trips to destinations throughout the western United States. Phil always loved a good adventure, and his 'girls' learned to love them, too.

They'd even gone river rafting one summer. *Imagine that,* Joan thought as she studied the photos of the three of them perched in their raft among a large group of people on a guided tour. She looked closely at her face and saw a bit of Sheila and a bit of Michelle looking back at her.

We sure did have some fun times, she thought as she sat back in her chair. "What should I do with all this?" she asked Thumper.

He looked up at her in eager anticipation of some announcement. When none came, he rested his head back down on his paws.

That evening she called Sheila and reported on her finds from the attic. "Do you think Michelle and Steve's pastor friend would like your father's sermon notes?"

"I don't know, Mom. We can ask."

"What should I do with all the old photos and your treasures from elementary school?" A long pause made her wonder if they'd lost their connection. "Sheila, are you still there?"

"Yeah. I'm here. Keep the photos for sure. I just don't know what to tell you about the rest of that stuff. It's nothing I have room for here in this little house. I guess you can toss it."

Joan knew her daughter was right. But it seemed so sad to throw away those memories. "Maybe I'll hold on to a few of the things," she said.

"Okay, but remember—you probably won't have a lot of storage space in your new place either, once you move up here."

By the end of the conversation, Sheila had persuaded her that she should come down in a couple of weeks and help her pack. "Who knows? Maybe I'll find a treasure or two that I decide to keep myself," she added.

"I hope so, honey. We've been holding onto these things for so long. It seems a shame to just toss the whole lot of it," Joan replied, hoping that her daughter would, indeed, want to keep a few things from her childhood home.

⁓

Sheila sighed as she hung up the phone.

"Everything okay?" Rick asked.

"I guess," she replied, gazing off into space.

"Sounds like she's doing some packing," he offered, to fill the silence.

Sheila turned and looked at him. "What?"

"Packing. It sounds like your mother's doing some packing." He reached over and took her hand. "You look worried."

"I am. A little. I just hate for her to be there alone."

He nodded. "Well, at least she's open to having you come down to help out." He released her hand, draped his

44

arm over her shoulder and pulled her close. "I'm going to miss you," he said as he kissed the side of her head.

Sheila leaned into him. Her heart swelled with love and gratitude. What an amazing thing to be in a new relationship at her age. She placed her hand on his leg and gave it a pat. "I promise I won't be gone for long."

"I'm going to hold you to that," he replied.

They sat nestled together for a few minutes. Then Sheila patted his leg again and stood up. "I'd better get to these dishes," she said, beginning to stack the plates on the coffee table in front of them from their dinner.

"I'll help you," Rick offered.

They carried their plates and glasses into the kitchen, and Sheila loaded them into the dishwasher while Rick leaned against the counter watching her.

"Want to go out for some dessert?" he asked as the last piece of silverware dropped into the basket.

"Seriously?"

"Sure. I could go for a hot fudge sundae right about now."

She laughed. "Where does your food go?" she asked, glancing at his trim waistline.

"I have secret compartments," he replied with a wink. "So what do you say? Are you game?"

"I can't believe we're doing this, but..."

"But you'll go."

"If you insist," she replied, smiling.

"Then we're off," he said as he reached for her hand.

Soon they were settled into a corner booth at The Igloo, a large hot fudge sundae perched in front of them, with two long-handled spoons reaching out from the mountain of ice cream and whipped topping. Rick pulled out one of them, filled it with all the delectable ingredients, and lifted it to Sheila's lips.

"Yum," she replied as she took a bite. "Now your turn." Following suit, she fed Rick his first bite, feeling like a kid back in high school.

As Rick wrapped his mouth around the mound of ice cream and fudge, a drip ran down his chin.

"Oops," Sheila said with a grin, grabbing a napkin and dabbing it away.

He leaned in and kissed her. Then holding his spoon up, he said, "Ready, set, go!" and dove into the sundae, quickly taking a bite. Sheila plunged her spoon into the frozen concoction and grabbed a bite for herself as well.

Three bites later, she put her spoon on her napkin and held up her hands in surrender. "Brain freeze," she said.

"Okay. I guess the rest is mine," he replied with a wink, pulling the bowl in front of himself.

"Not on your life," she said, pulling it back to the middle. "Just give me a minute."

He looked at her and grinned, not saying a word, his eyes fixed on her face.

"What? Do I have ice cream somewhere?" she asked, dabbing her napkin on her lips. "Why are you staring at me?"

He shook his head. "You don't have any idea how beautiful you are, do you?"

She felt the heat rush to her face. "You're just on a sugar high," she replied.

"No. I'm just wondering how I did life before you."

She studied his face. A hint of sorrow in his eyes caught her by surprise. "Are you okay?" she asked softly.

He nodded. "Yeah." After pausing, he added, "Thanks for giving me a chance. I mean it."

Sheila's mind flashed back to the first time she'd heard about Rick Chambers. He was Michelle's anthropology professor and took pride in rattling the beliefs of the Christian students in his classes. A staunch atheist after his mother's early death, he'd felt it was his duty to shake the Christians on campus from their fantasies about God.

On the last day of class, Michelle had given him a letter explaining how she came to her faith through her father's desperate suicide attempt. She'd used the letter to invite him to church. But it wasn't until years later when Sheila and Michelle had run into Rick at the local Coffee Stop, that he'd actually decided to take her up on the invitation. Now, nearly a year later, he was a changed man, seeking God, studying scripture, and drawing Sheila into his world.

"You don't regret it, do you?" His voice broke her thoughts.

"Hmmm? Regret what?" she asked.

"Giving me a chance."

She looked into his eyes and saw a vulnerability she knew he rarely showed anyone. Placing her hand on his, she replied, "Not for one second."

⚜

As Sheila slipped back inside her house later that night, Rick's goodbye kiss still warm on her lips, she caught the tail end of the phone ringing. *I wonder if that was Mom again,* she thought, hurrying into the kitchen to check the caller ID. It showed Michelle's name.

Picking up the receiver, she dialed.

Michelle's voice immediately greeted her, "Hi, Mom."

"Hi, honey. Sorry I missed your call. I just got home."

"Really? Where were you?" she asked, sounding a little concerned.

"Just out with Rick."

"Oh, I thought you two were eating in tonight."

"We did. Then he got inspired to go to The Igloo for a sundae."

"You guys are getting pretty serious aren't you?" her daughter asked.

"Because we went out for a sundae?" Sheila teased.

"No, because you spend almost every waking moment together."

Sheila paused for a moment. Was Michelle feeling like she was neglecting her or the grandkids? Before she could ask, Michelle spoke, almost as if reading her mind.

"I'm just kidding, Mom. I'm glad you two are happy."

Sheila smiled. "Thanks. So how are things with you?"

"Crazy busy with school. You know—lesson plans, getting to know the new kids, plus getting Caleb and Madison launched into their new school year, too." She paused and then added wistfully, "Sure wish Steve and I had more dates like you and Rick."

"Maybe in a few weeks, things will settle down and you can get more time together," Sheila suggested.

"Yeah. Maybe. I was even thinking I might try to arrange for a weekend away, just the two of us. Would you be able to stay with the kids?"

"Depends on when it is. I'm heading down to Mariposa in a couple of weeks to help your grandmother pack."

"Speaking of Grandma, she called me tonight," Michelle said.

"Really?"

"Yeah. She wanted to talk to me about some old family pictures and memorabilia she found in the attic or somewhere. She said that you told her she probably wouldn't have room for it at her new place." Michelle hesitated and then added, "She sounded really sad, Mom."

Sheila's heart was pierced. Maybe she shouldn't have been so hasty in making that statement. Before she could respond, Michelle continued, "I really think we should go easy with Grandma about getting rid of stuff. This whole move is going to be a huge step for her."

Her daughter's wisdom hit home. "You're right. I should have waited until I got down there and then sorted through stuff with her myself. I'm sure I can find room somewhere for the things that she really treasures."

"She asked me if I wanted any of her furniture or pictures on the wall or china or anything."

"You know, Michelle, maybe it will be easier for her to part with some of her things if she knows they've found good homes with family. If there is anything you'd want, just let me know. I can set it aside for you when we're packing."

"Good idea, Mom. Why don't you figure out what you think she can keep and then text me pictures of the stuff that won't fit into her new place. I know you are planning to store some of her stuff in your garage while she's staying with you. I can ask Steve if we can park our cars out on the driveway so more stuff can be stored here, too."

"That would be great, honey. Thanks."

"Sure. No problem. Are you and Rick still coming over for an early dinner on Sunday? The kids are eager to see you again."

"We're planning on it," Sheila replied, the heaviness in her heart over her mom's difficulties lifting as she shifted her mind to Rick and the grandkids.

"And you're bringing the salad?" Michelle asked.

"Yep. And dessert."

"Great! We'll see you Sunday."

As Sheila hung up the phone, thoughts of her mother once again flooded her mind. *Dear Lord, please help Mom get through this move. And give me wisdom so that I can be supportive and compassionate in the process.*

CHAPTER SEVEN

As the time for Sheila's arrival got closer, Joan found herself caught up in a myriad of emotions. Not wanting to be hurried through her sorting process once her daughter arrived, she tried to go through as many closets and cupboards as she could.

Each day brought a slew of reminders of Phil. And Joan's heart ached deeply with every image of him that crossed her mind. Sometimes she'd close her eyes, wrap her arms around herself and imagine that he was hugging her.

What would it be like to leave their home and never return? At least here, she could sometimes feel his presence in the memories. When she lived in a new place, a home he'd never even been in, would she lose the little bit of him that remained? Sometimes she even felt fearful that she'd forget what he looked like or the sound of his voice, bringing on increasing anxiety about the move.

Am I ready for this, Lord? Will I miss Phil all the more if I move?

Although her morning quiet times alone with God were becoming critically important to Joan, she still yearned for Phil's calming voice and the way he used to lift their petitions toward heaven. She loved the Lord with all her heart, and sometimes His presence seemed to fill the room in ways that brought great comfort and peace. But she realized how important Phil's spiritual leadership had been in their home and marriage.

She found herself trying to grasp the idea of being the bride of Christ. A concept that never held the same desperate appeal in the past as it did now.

Phil spent his life in communion with God. It didn't matter if he was walking the dog, pulling weeds in the garden, or preaching a sermon. Joan needed that now— God's presence in her life, moment-by-moment, as she learned to navigate the waters of widowhood.

Sitting on the porch swing one morning, she set aside her devotional book, closed her eyes, and began sharing the depths of her heart. "Dear Jesus, I don't know how to do this life now. I'm not sure I can make it without Phil. I feel so alone, and I honestly don't know why I'm still here. I've done my best to be a good wife and mother. And I'm thankful for the chance to do that. But now? What does life hold for me now? I'm just an old woman without a purpose." A tear slipped from her eye, and then another one, until she let go and sobbed. "Please, God, would you just take me home?"

And then it happened.

Without opening her eyes, she suddenly knew that she was not alone on that porch swing. She could feel Jesus' presence and her heart could hear Him speak.

You are not alone.

She froze, afraid to move, and desperately wanting Him to stay this close, this very real and present.

Await My plans, Joan. Pray and prepare for a new purpose.

A new purpose? At her age? All she could do was to nod her head. "I will, Lord."

She spent the next few minutes with her eyes closed as she soaked in the love of God. Then, drying her tears and gazing out over the property, her focus lit on the shed.

It was Phil's special spot. He'd made it into a little office, and he loved to work on his projects there. Before he died, he'd been working on one, but he'd never gotten the chance to show it to her. And she'd forgotten all about it in the wake of his medical needs when the cancer overtook his body.

"Should I go look, Lord?" she asked aloud, feeling torn between her curiosity and the pact she and Phil had made about her never peeking before he was finished. Would she find a half completed project of some kind that would only break her heart all the more?

I will go with you, Joan.

She marveled at the closeness of God. It filled her spirit to the point that she wondered if she could even contain it. Rising to her feet, she could almost hear the soft slapping of Jesus' sandals beside her as she made her way to the shed. Her hand froze for a minute on the handle. Then she said, "I'm going in, Phil," and she turned the knob.

In the middle of the floor, a large box stared at her. Scrawled across it, in familiar handwriting, were the words "Do not open until Christmas." On top of the box was an envelope with her name in Phil's cursive. Her hand shook as she pulled out the letter inside. Carefully unfolding it, she sank into the chair at his desk and began to read.

My darling Jo,

By the time you read this, I will be gone. But it is important for you to know that my heart is knit with yours forever. And if it is possible for me to be part of that great cloud of witnesses from Hebrews 12 cheering you on to your own finish line, you'd better believe I will be in the very front row with my hands lifted in the air and my voice proclaiming your victory in the final stretch of the race.

Through all the years we've been together, it has been my greatest privilege to be your husband. I've cherished every moment God has given me in that calling. Although you had to share me with a congregation, please know that being by your side was always my favorite place.

53

As I write this, I'm getting more and more eager to see Jesus. It's exciting to know that it will be soon. But I want to tell you that leaving you is the hardest thing I have ever had to do. I've spent many hours out here fervently praying for your protection and asking God to guide your future.

Sheila and the kids have told me how much they'd like you to move near them when I'm gone. I know it will be hard for you to leave this home. We've got a lifetime of memories here. It's been a good life, too. Watching our daughter grow up, get married, and have her own family. So many happy times, as well as a few sad ones that reminded us to cling to each other and God.

I hope you'll seriously consider moving, Jo. I think it would be good for you to be near family. It's a blessing to have that opportunity. Don't worry about the memories. They don't live in this house. They live in our hearts.

Since I won't be here for Christmas, I wanted to put a little something together for you and the kids. You know the rules. No peeking and no opening before the actual day. Trent helped me quite a bit with this project, so you should thank him when you get a chance. He's a good kid, Jo. He promised he'd help you out, so I hope you'll call on him if you need a hand.

And keep an eye on old Thumper for me. I'm glad you'll have him standing guard here over the property. But if you move up to Sandy Cove, I hope you'll think about giving him to Caleb. That boy really loves our old dog. And maybe you can get one of those kittens you were always trying to talk me into.

All right, my dear. I'm done with my rambling. I'll be watching for you on the other side.

All my love,

Phil

Joan clutched the letter to her chest and cried once again. Tears of gratitude for one more communication from her husband, tears of relief for his continued guidance in her moving decision, and tears of mourning for a man she could no longer hold in her arms.

She leaned over and gave the box a nudge. It wasn't very heavy, in spite of its large size. "I wonder what could be in here?" she said to the walls of the shed.

CHAPTER EIGHT

Sheila called a few days later. "Mom, I've found a really cute apartment in a senior complex called Shoreline Manor. It's near my house."

Now that Joan felt Phil's support and encouragement for the move, she wanted to hear all about it. "Tell me everything, dear. Have you been inside?"

"Yes. I went yesterday afternoon. I would have called last night, but Rick and I had tickets for a concert, and it was pretty late by the time we got home."

"Okay, well I'm glad you've seen the inside. What's it like?" Joan said, reaching over and stroking Thumper, who was pressing against her.

"The grounds are beautiful, Mom. Lots of flowerbeds and walkways with large pines and a few mature maple trees. They even have a vegetable garden that the residents maintain and harvest."

"Sounds really nice. Your father would have loved the vegetable garden idea," she added. Thumper nudged her again. "What about dogs? Are they allowed in the apartments?"

There was a pause at the other end. "Well, yes and no. They do allow dogs, but only breeds under 25 pounds, so I'm afraid Thumper wouldn't qualify."

Joan could feel the dog's cold nose prodding her hand to pet him. She looked lovingly down at him and then recalled the words in Phil's letter—'I hope you'll think about giving him to Caleb'. "You know, Sheila, I've actually been considering asking Michelle if it would be alright to give Thumper to Caleb. He's taken to this old guy so well, and Thumper seems more like a pup around him."

"Really? I think that would be a great idea, Mom. Caleb would love to have a dog, and he still talks about the time Thumper stayed with them when you were here for Dad's memorial."

"Okay, maybe that will work out well. So, do you have a brochure or something you can send me about this apartment complex?" Joan's heart wrestled within, pulling her in two directions. Fear of change and loss left part of her clinging to home, but another part was beginning to get excited about a new place near her family.

"Yes, and it even has a DVD in the handout that you can watch on your television to see a little movie tour. I'll put it in the mail today," she promised. "Call me after you get a chance to look at everything. If you like what you see, I'll have them hold a spot for you and will come down to help you pack."

"Okay, dear." Joan paused for a moment and wondered if she should tell Sheila about her discovery in the shed. But the timing didn't seem right. She decided to wait until her daughter arrived to help her pack. *It will be better to share the surprise with her in person.*

After Sheila hung up the phone, she felt a wave of peace and gratitude wash over her. *Mom sounds much more upbeat about the move. I wonder what changed her mind.* She flipped through the brochure for Shoreline Manor and read the section about pricing and leases.

I'd better get over there today and see about having them hold an apartment. Maybe Rick will go with me.

She picked up the phone again and called Rick's number. Voicemail. She left a brief message explaining the reason for her call and asking him to call back. Then she remembered he'd said something about a faculty meeting at the university later in the day that might run into dinnertime. She glanced at the clock. Half past four.

Maybe I'd better just go by myself, she thought. As she was gathering her purse, keys, and sweater, the phone rang.

"Hi, Mom," Michelle's voice said. "What are you up to?"

"I was just about to head over to Shoreline Manor."

"What's that?"

"Didn't I tell you about it on Sunday?"

"Oh, yeah. The senior apartment complex by the beach."

"Yeah. That's it."

"Did you talk to Grandma about it?"

"I did. We just got off the phone. She sounded interested, and I told her I'd go see if I could have them hold a unit for her."

"Can I come along?" Michelle asked.

Sheila was pleasantly surprised. "Sure! But do you have time? I mean it's getting close to dinner."

"No problem. Steve said he'd pick up Chinese on his way home. Madison's doing homework and Caleb is watching television, so I'm sure I can go with you for a little bit."

"The kids will be okay alone?"

"Yeah. We've started leaving them for short time periods. Madison's almost thirteen, you know."

Sheila sighed. "I can hardly believe it. But yes, your dad and I used to leave you and Tim home alone when you were her age."

"So do you want to swing by here and pick me up?"

"Sure. I'm just about to leave. I'll see you in a few minutes."

As they toured the grounds, Michelle tried to imagine her grandmother living at Shoreline Manor. Surveying the grounds, her mind traveled back in time to a collection of treasured memories of her grandparents and their home. She could see Grandpa Phil sitting beside her on the top step of the front porch as Grandma Joan called to them from the kitchen.

"Come try this apple pie," her voice beckoned from the past.

Michelle remembered watching her mother on the porch swing, Michelle's baby brother in her arms as they gently swung back and forth.

Grandma and Grandpa's house was always a place of adventure and family fun. Over the years, a variety of dogs had come and gone, but there was always one following Grandpa around the property or running after a ball or Frisbee.

And she could still feel the warmth of the summer sun and the delicious smells that wafted out the kitchen window.

Yep. It was one of her very favorite spots in the world.

Even after Michelle was grown and had kids of her own, she still loved going to Mariposa and spending time at their home. There was something so very peaceful about the place.

As she looked around Shoreline Manor, she had to admit it was pretty peaceful there, too. But in a different way. A hushed, quiet kind of peacefulness that lacked the hominess of her grandparents' spread.

"Do you think Grandma will feel at home here?" she asked her mother.

"I sure hope so, honey. She needs to be near family now, and no matter how much I try to convince her to move in with me, she will not even consider it," Sheila replied, adding, "Let's go look inside one of the apartments." She pointed to a building off to the right. "I think the one on the ground floor over there would be the best location."

They walked along the paved path, winding through sprawling emerald lawns and beautiful flowerbeds. Everything looked perfectly manicured. But to Michelle, it seemed almost too perfect. There was something about the dirt and rocky flowerbeds of her grandparents place that spoke of God, not man. The one consolation was the sound of the nearby surf that Michelle knew her grandmother would love.

As they met up with the woman who would be showing them the apartment, Michelle tried to keep an upbeat attitude. "Beautiful grounds," she said to the woman with a smile.

"We try to keep it well groomed," the woman replied. "But the residents' favorite patch is the vegetable garden around back. And, of course, many residents keep their own potted and hanging plants on their patios."

"I'd love to see the vegetable garden," Michelle said, her spirits picking up as she imagined her grandmother poking around in a garden again.

The woman smiled warmly. "Yes, we'll be sure to go over there after you two take a look at the apartment." She fingered the keys on her key ring until she found the correct one for the front door. After she unlocked the bolt, she opened the door and stepped back, gesturing for Michelle and her mother to enter.

The smell of new carpet and paint filled Michelle's nostrils.

"Here, let me open some windows," their guide said, as if reading Michelle's thoughts. "They just finished preparing this unit for new occupancy," she added cheerfully.

As she drew back the curtains and opened the windows, the sound of the waves and the smell of the ocean rushed into the living room. "Now that's better," she said to Michelle and her mother.

Sheila walked over and looked out the window. "Come and see the view," she said.

Michelle joined her, and they gazed out over the lawn and then to the sea. Off in the distance, they could see the lighthouse perched on a rocky jetty with the park beside it.

"It's a beautiful location," Michelle agreed.

"I wouldn't mind living here myself," her mother added with a smile.

"Would you like to see the rest of the rooms?" their tour guide asked.

"Definitely," Michelle replied.

They went into the kitchen next. Although it wasn't anything like her grandmother's old oak cabinetry and tile counters, the crisp white woodwork and sandy colored granite looked very inviting and beachy. Michelle particularly liked the glass front cabinet doors that flanked the window. "Grandma's dishes will look nice in these," she commented, noticing her mother's smile in response.

Next the woman opened a door that led into a pantry.

"Wow, I was thinking that was a door into a garage," Michelle said. "That's quite a big pantry for an apartment."

"There are no attached garages," the woman replied. "I hope that won't be a problem."

"No problem at all," Sheila replied. "Mom doesn't have a car."

Leaving the kitchen, they toured through the dining area, the two bedrooms, the master bath, and the guest bathroom. Everything was spotless. Each bedroom had a sliding glass door leading out to a small patio, and a larger patio off the living area looked out to the ocean. Although the patios were empty, Michelle noticed how cute others in the building looked with their porch furniture, gliders, and planters.

Maybe Grandma will be happy here after all, she thought. Then she turned and asked, "Can we see the vegetable garden now?"

Her mother laughed. "You really seem interested in that."

"I just think it would be fun for Grandma since she's always had her own garden."

"Yes, but remember that Grandpa did much of the work in those gardens," her mother added.

After locking up the apartment, they headed out to see the rest of the grounds as well as the vegetable patch. When they got to it, Michelle was surprised to see how large it was. There were several residents working the garden—pulling weeds, planting seeds, and hoeing the ground.

Their guide introduced them to each person by name. Michelle was impressed with the family friendliness between the woman and the folks working in the garden. They bantered back and forth a bit about the progress of the vegetables, and Michelle noticed the woman asked each resident something about his or her family as well.

"These folks mean the world to me," she told Michelle and her mother as they moved along on their tour. "We're all 'family' here," she added.

Soon they were heading into the office, where Sheila would get more details on the lease of the apartment.

"Mom, would you mind if I went back to the vegetable garden to chat with some of the residents who are working out there?" Michelle asked.

Her mother smiled. "Not at all. Go right ahead. I'll call your cell phone when I'm ready to leave."

Michelle took a shortcut across the property and was glad to see that a couple of people were still out in the garden. She overheard two of them discussing their tomato crops. "Take some of these back to your apartment," one man offered as he handed a couple of his ripe tomatoes to a woman weeding nearby.

"Thanks, Hank," she said with a nod as she stood and took them from him. After placing them in her basket, she brushed the dirt from her hands, and told him goodbye. "Coming with me, Millie?" she asked another woman nearby, who had her own basket full of vegetables.

"Yes, indeed," her friend replied.

As soon as the two women had left, Hank turned to her and offered her a tomato. "Would you like one, young lady?"

She smiled and accepted his offer. "It looks delicious."

He grinned and nodded. "A good crop this year. So what brings you here to Shoreline Manor?"

"We're looking at an apartment for my grandmother. She may be moving here from California," she began, and then added, "My grandfather passed away not too long ago."

Hank nodded again. "I'm sorry to hear that. Lost my own Helen six months ago. We'd been married for sixty-two years." His voice dropped, as did his smile.

Michelle tried to imagine what it would be like to be married to Steve that long and then be alone. "I'm sure you must miss her very much," she offered.

"Yup. But I know I'll see her again someday," he said, gazing off toward the ocean and nodding to himself. Then he cleared his throat and turned his attention back to Michelle. "So tell me about your grandmother."

"Okay. Her name is Joan. She's a wonderful person, and she was very supportive of my grandfather's ministry as a pastor. She's pretty spry and a little opinionated. And she's a great cook," she added with a grin.

"So, you say she's going to be moving here?" he asked.

"I think so. It'll be hard for her to leave the home where she and my grandfather lived for most of their lives. But we all feel it's important for her to be near family now.

She hurt her arm not too long ago, and we were all so far away that she ended up in the hospital alone overnight before my mom could get down there."

He nodded. "It's a big adjustment to move at our age, but I've got to say that the people here are really friendly. I mean not just the people who work here, but the residents, too. That helps."

"I'll bet," she replied. "Hey, thanks for talking to me. And for the tomato," she added, holding it up with a smile.

"My pleasure. I'll keep an eye out for your grandmother," he said. "Maybe I can help her get a patch of her own going here," he added as he gestured to a plot of dirt next to his tomato vine.

"That would be great. I'm sure she'd love the help," Michelle told him. And for the first time, she thought just maybe her grandmother would be okay in this new place.

After dropping Michelle off at home and putting a Shoreline Manor brochure in the mail to her mother down in Mariposa, Sheila went home and fixed herself some tea. Putting her feet up on the coffee table and sipping the cinnamon flavored brew, she looked through all the paperwork once again.

It was tough trying to imagine her mother living there. But it was just as tough to think of her on her own down in that big old house with all that property to maintain.

Sheila hated the idea of selling her childhood home. Most of her memories of her father were there as well as countless other moments in her life's history. But there was no way she could imagine keeping the place, paying for all its upkeep and taxes, and still being able to afford a unit at Shoreline Manor.

Dear Lord, please make this clear to all of us. If Mom is supposed to move up here, give her a good feeling about it. She rested her head back against the soft pillows on the couch and dozed off, only to be awakened a half-hour later by the phone ringing.

It was Michelle telling her Steve was home with the dinner and wondering if she'd like to join them.

"I don't think so, honey. But thanks. I'm kind of beat. Think I'll just have a quiet evening at home."

"Okay," she replied. "And Mom?"

"Yes?"

"I think Grandma will be fine at Shoreline Manor."

"You do?"

"Yeah. I really do."

After they hung up, Sheila felt a little better. Then the doorbell rang, and she found Rick standing on the front porch with a bouquet of flowers. Suddenly she didn't feel so tired after all.

CHAPTER NINE

Joan received the brochure for Shoreline Manor two days later. She carried it in from the mailbox and studied the glossy pages filled with attractive photos of the grounds and the interiors of the apartments. The units looked bright and cheerful with modern appliances and countertops. But they also looked very small, much smaller than the place she'd called home for nearly sixty years.

As she gazed around her front room, she wondered aloud, "Where am I going to put all my treasures?" She'd planned to get rid of some of her things. Maybe even half. But these tiny residences would require her to give up most of the items she'd collected over the years. Items that were dear to her.

Again anxiety wrapped its icy fingers around her heart. Maybe she should just stay in Mariposa. She put the brochure on the side table. *I'll watch the DVD later.*

That night, as she was getting ready for bed, Thumper began barking by the front window. She pulled on her robe and headed out to see what he was so upset about, fear fighting to have its way with her.

By the time she got to the dog, he had his front paws on the window ledge and his lips were curled in a menacing expression. His loud barking was unnerving, and she reached for his collar to guide him away from the window. Somehow in the process, she lost her footing and fell, landing on her right hand and hip.

Immediately a sharp pain shot through her right arm and shoulder. She cried out in pain, and the sound startled Thumper enough that he stopped barking and faced her, panting and beginning to lick at her face.

At first, all Joan could do was moan. Pushing the dog away with her left hand, she managed to roll onto her knees, cradling her right arm to her chest. Then crawling to the couch, she used her good arm to pull herself up. As she sat down, she reached over and grabbed the phone. Her phone book was in the kitchen, so she called the only number she knew by heart.

"Mom?" Sheila's voice answered.

Joan felt like she was about to lose her dinner. "Yes. It's me," she replied, waves of nausea adding to the distress of her pain. "I'm hurt."

"What? What happened?"

"I…I fell."

"How badly are you hurt?"

Joan took a breath. The pain in her arm brought tears to her eyes. "Pretty bad. I think I broke my arm."

"Okay. Listen, Mom. You've got to hang up the phone and call 911. Okay?"

She nodded and took a deep breath. "Okay."

"And call me back after they get there."

"I will."

Joan did as Sheila instructed, and five minutes later a fire truck and paramedic van pulled into the driveway. Thumper went crazy as the paramedics knocked on the front door. Forcing herself to her feet, Joan somehow managed to shuffle over and unlock the door as tears streamed down her cheeks.

Immediately the paramedics went to work helping her to the couch again and beginning their examination.

"I need to call my daughter back," she said as they prepared to take her to the hospital.

"What's your daughter's name and number, Ma'am?" one of the nice young men asked. He wrote down what she told him and then promised to call Sheila himself. "You'll be able to talk to her once you get settled at the hospital," he promised.

Four hours and several X-rays later, Joan got the news. "You have a fracture of the radius and a pretty bad sprain in your shoulder. We'll leave you in a temporary splint and sling for now until the swelling goes down. But eventually you will need a cast from your hand to above your elbow. Do you live alone?" he asked.

"Yes. Except for my dog," she replied, hoping Thumper was managing all right without her.

"Then I think we'll keep you overnight for observation. We've given you some pretty strong pain medication, and it'll be best for you to just sleep for a while. Would you like to call your daughter now? The paramedics mentioned they'd talked to her and she was eager to hear from you."

Joan nodded.

"Okay, I'll have the nurse help you get settled into a room and then you can give her a call."

By the time Joan could call Sheila, it was well after midnight. She explained what the doctor had told her and that she was staying at the hospital overnight.

"I'm coming down tomorrow," her daughter said. "I'm not sure what time I'll arrive, but it will probably be late in the day or maybe even after dinner. It depends on which flight I can get from here. Is the nurse there with you?"

"No."

"Okay, I'll call the hospital after we hang up and see if they can keep you until I get there."

"What about Thumper?" Joan asked, worried about the dog trapped in the house.

"I'll try to get a hold of Trent. They have your house key, right?"

"Yes."

"Okay. I'm sure someone there can go feed him in the morning and put him out."

Joan was feeling so exhausted she could barely keep her eyes open. "I think I'd better hang up and try to sleep," she said.

"Good idea, Mom. I'll see you tomorrow. Don't worry about anything, okay?"

"Okay, dear." She reached over and hung up the phone, then slipped into a deep slumber.

Adrenaline surged through Sheila as she began calling airlines for a reservation. *I've got to get there,* she thought, her head spinning with concern and questions. Thankfully, she was able to grab a spot on the first flight out of Portland in the morning.

As soon as she got off the phone with the airline, she dialed Michelle.

"Mom? Are you okay?" her daughter asked, clearly concerned about the late night call.

"I'm fine, honey. But Grandma's in the hospital."

"What? What happened?"

Sheila explained all that she knew about her mother's injury and then added, "I'm flying down there in the morning."

"Okay. Do you want me to take a half day off from school to take you to the airport?" Michelle asked.

"Let me call Rick, and I'll get back to you on that. In the meantime, just please be praying for your grandmother. She must be feeling really alone right now."

"I will, Mom. Call me back after you talk to Rick."

Before dialing Rick's number, Sheila paused to pray. *Please, Lord, be with Mom. Give her peace and ease her pain. Help her sleep tonight and be okay until I get there.*

70

Rick answered on the second ring. "Well, this is a nice surprise," he said. "I was just thinking about you."

His voice soothed her spirit and helped her regain her composure. "I've got a little emergency here, Rick."

"Really? What's up?"

"It's Mom. She fell and ended up in the hospital with a broken arm."

"Oh, no. Is there anything I can do? Do you want me to come over and we'll drive down there?"

Sheila's heart swelled with gratitude and love. "That's really sweet. But I arranged a flight for first thing in the morning. Is there any chance you could drive me to the airport?"

"Of course. What time do you want me to pick you up?"

Suddenly a wave of emotion overtook Sheila and she felt like she was going to cry.

"Sheila? Are you still there?" he asked.

Taking a deep breath, she steadied herself and replied, "Yes. I'm here. Just feeling a little emotional."

"Do you want me to come over?" He sounded concerned.

"No. It's okay. I need to focus and pack. And then I'd better try to get some sleep," she replied, while her heart cried out, *Come.*

Rick cleared his throat. "I'm coming over. I promise I won't get in the way of your packing, and I won't stay long."

A smile crept across Sheila's face, as one lone tear slipped down her cheek. "Thanks," she said softly.

Ten minutes later, he was at her door. Without a word, she walked into his open arms, leaning her head against his chest as he held her close.

"It'll be okay," he said softly, and she nodded. His calm assurance penetrated her being, and she silently thanked

God for this man and the unexpected blessing he brought into her life.

CHAPTER TEN

As Joan opened her eyes the next morning, she found herself in an unfamiliar setting. Trying to push up to a sitting position, the pain sliced through her right arm.

"Here, let me help you," a voice said. Immediately a nurse was at her side, using the bed's remote control to elevate Joan's head. She must have looked pretty confused, because the nurse began explaining, "You're in the hospital. You took a fall last night and broke your wrist and sprained your shoulder."

Joan nodded, everything coming back to her. "I remember. I just feel so drugged right now."

"It's the pain medication. Here, have some water. And then we'll talk about your breakfast." The nurse held a cup of water for her, moving the straw so it was easy for Joan to take a drink.

She hadn't realized how thirsty she was until after the first swallow. She emptied the cup and then asked for assistance to use the restroom. What an ordeal that proved to be without the use of her right arm! Life was going to be challenging for a while.

Next she was presented with a breakfast menu. Her stomach felt a little queasy, but the nurse assured her that food would be helpful. After ordering a poached egg and toast, she settled back against the pillow and rested. She ate as much of it as she could, and then dozed on and off for the rest of the morning.

Around noon, Sheila arrived. Seeing her daughter standing in the doorway brought such relief and joy. Loneliness had been her companion too long. She needed family.

Sheila leaned over and gave her a kiss on the cheek. "How are you feeling, Mom?"

"Good, now that you are here," she replied with a smile. As she reached to take Sheila's hand, she winced again from the pain. Even using her left side seemed to somehow trigger pain on the right.

"Let's see if we can get you something for that pain," Sheila said.

"I think they're already giving me whatever they can. It's just going to take a few days before I start feeling better."

Her daughter nodded. "I'll go talk to the nurse and find out if I can take you home this afternoon."

When she returned, a doctor was with her. "I've been discussing your break with your daughter, Mrs. Walker, and I think it's fine for you to go home as long as she will be there to take care of you. I've explained that we set the bone, but you'll need to be seen by an orthopedic specialist later in the week when the swelling has gone down to get a regular cast."

"Thank you, doctor," Joan replied.

He handed Sheila some paperwork to sign regarding care instructions and follow up. "Here's the name of a good orthopedic surgeon," he added, handing her a business card.

Sheila thanked him. As soon as he'd left the room, the nurse and Sheila worked together to get Joan out of bed and dressed. "I have a rental car parked in the lot," Sheila told the nurse, who was helping Joan into a wheelchair. "I'll go bring it around to the front and meet you there."

"I feel silly in this chair," Joan said. "I can walk. Really."

"Hospital regulations," the nurse replied with a smile. "Enjoy the free ride."

When they got to the front of the hospital, Sheila was waiting with a snazzy red compact car. "What do you think, Mom?" she asked with a wink.

"It suits you, dear," she replied, returning her daughter's smile. *Thank you, Lord, for bringing her down here.*

As they pulled into Joan's driveway, Thumper ran to greet them, Trent close on his heels.

"I was just letting him out," the boy explained. "He took off as soon as he saw the car coming."

Although Thumper seemed happy to see them, Joan noticed he looked in the car one last time after they'd gotten out. *Probably still looking for Phil,* she thought sadly.

"Would you like to join us for a bite to eat?" Sheila asked Trent. "Mom missed lunch, so I'm going to fix her something."

"No thanks. I've got to get to football practice. Just stopped by for a minute to let the dog out." He picked up his bike that was lying on the grass and hopped on. "See you later, Mrs. Walker. Let me know if you need anything else." He waved as he took off down the driveway.

"Let's get you inside, Mom," Sheila said, taking her by the left elbow and helping her up the porch steps.

Soon Joan was propped up on the couch, her right arm supported on a pillow resting on her lap. Sheila made some lemonade and sandwiches and they sat together in the living room eating and visiting.

"So how're Michelle and the kids doing?" Joan wanted to know.

"They're fine. Busy with school, of course. Caleb's got quite a big class this year, but he really likes his teacher, so

I guess he's happy. Madison started at Magnolia Middle School, so she and Michelle are commuting together this year. It's a big step for Maddie, going from class to class and having a locker. But she seems to be adjusting well, although Michelle said she barely acknowledges her in the hallways. I guess it's a little tough being at the same school where your mother is a teacher."

"I can imagine. I remember you at that age. Your father said you made him drop you off a block away from school each morning."

Sheila laughed. "Yeah." Then her smile fell, and Joan knew she was thinking about Phil and how much they both missed him.

"So how long do you plan to stay, sweetheart? I really appreciate you coming down to get me out of the hospital, but I don't want to drag you away from your life and all that's happening with Rick these days."

"You heard the doctor, Mother. I will stay here as long as you need help. Rick understands. We wouldn't have it any other way."

Again, relief washed over Joan. She didn't want to be a burden, but she was also wondering how she could possibly manage alone right now.

"You know, Mom, before we know it, the holidays will be upon us. Maybe you should think about just coming home with me after we get your arm set in a cast. I'd love to have you there, and it would give you more of a chance to get to know Rick. Plus, you could go visit Shoreline Manor and see it for yourself. Then after Christmas, maybe we can move you up there permanently."

Joan let the idea roll around in her head for a few moments before answering. Go a voice within urged. "Okay."

"Okay?" Sheila looked surprised. "Just like that?"

"Just like that." Joan smiled. Then she thought about the dog. "What about Thumper?"

"Michelle will keep him for now."

"I hate to put that responsibility on her at such a busy time, what with school in full gear."

"It'll be fine, Mom. Really. And Caleb will be ecstatic."

"If you say so," she replied hesitantly.

"Okay, then it's settled. After we get you in to see the orthopedic doctor, we'll head up to Sandy Cove."

That night, as Sheila was getting ready for bed, she retrieved her phone from her purse to call Rick. The screen was black, and she realized she'd forgotten to turn it back on after the flight that morning. As she powered it up, she saw multiple voicemail messages in her inbox. Three were from Michelle, and four from Rick.

Michelle had called before school, during her lunch break, and after she'd gotten home. "Please call me, Mom. I'm dying to hear how Grandma's doing."

Sheila hit the autodial button for her daughter as she settled back against the pillows at the headboard of the bed.

"Mom? I've been trying to reach you all day. How's Grandma?"

"She'll be okay, honey. But I'm going to need to stay here for a while. We've got to go to the orthopedic doctor in a few days, and then I'm hoping to bring her home with me."

"Do you need me to do anything while you're gone?"

"No. I think everything will be fine at my house. I'll let you know about our travel plans after we see the doctor. It's possible we may need a ride home from the airport."

"Okay. Just let me know. I can take time off if you need me to," she said.

"Thanks. I'll keep you posted."

"Tell Grandma I love her and we're praying for her."

"I will. She'll appreciate that."

As soon as she got off the line with Michelle, Sheila called Rick. She filled him in on the day and her plans to bring her mother back to Sandy Cove as soon as possible.

"If you need me to drive down there to get you two, just let me know," he offered.

"Actually, that might just be the best solution," Sheila replied. "We'll need to bring the dog up, too, and arranging a flight for him is one more challenge."

"Then it's settled," he said. "I'll plan on going down. Do you think you'll be ready to travel this weekend?"

"I hope so. We'll see the specialist on Thursday. If he clears her to go, I'd like to get home."

"Okay, I'll keep the weekend open, and you can let me know."

"Rick?"

"Yeah?

She paused. "I don't know how to thank you for all this."

"It's my pleasure, sweetheart. Really."

Sweetheart. That was the first time he'd used that term when talking to her. *I could get used to this,* she thought joyfully.

CHAPTER ELEVEN

Each day that week, Joan's pain got more and more manageable and she was able to wean herself from the pain medication. Sheila was a great help to her. Every daily task now required assistance, and Joan was so thankful her daughter was there to meet every need—helping with bathing, toileting, dressing and undressing, meals, as well as packing for their upcoming trip back to Sandy Cove. Sheila even set up an arrangement with Trent to keep an eye on the house and keep up with the yard by doing some watering and mowing.

What would I do without her, Lord? Joan asked one day as she sat on the porch watching Sheila watering a brown spot on the lawn. *You are so faithful to provide for my every need. Phil would be so proud of her if he could see how much she's helped me this week.*

As she continued to gaze out over the yard, she noticed Thumper lying down in front of the shed. Her first thought was of how she wished she could explain to the dog that Phil was not coming back. Then another thought hit her. *The shed! I almost forgot to tell her about the box in the shed!*

"Sheila!"

Her daughter looked her way. "Yeah?"

"I almost forgot something very important that we need to take back to Sandy Cove with us," Joan replied.

Sheila turned off the hose and walked up onto the porch. "What is it?"

"It's in the shed. It's a box of Christmas gifts your father put together before...before he died," she said, forcing out the final words.

"You're kidding." Sheila looked stunned.

"No. I found it a little while back."

"Why didn't you tell me?" her daughter asked.

"I wanted to surprise you, just like he surprised me when I found it."

"Wow. When did he have time to do that?"

"I really don't know, honey, except that he and Trent worked out there for a few weeks before hospice set up his bed in the front room. He never made it back there after that," she added wistfully. "At the time, I'd asked him what he was working on. But he just said, 'You'll find out' and made me promise not to peek." Joan paused and looked off into space, Phil's face and voice visiting her memory with sharp clarity.

Then she continued. "When I started sorting through things to get ready to pack to move, I remembered the shed. As soon as I opened the door, I saw the box in the middle of the floor. There was a letter on top."

"A letter?"

"Yes. From your father. Do you want to see it?"

Sheila nodded.

"It's on my nightstand."

Sheila disappeared and returned a few minutes later. "Are you sure it's okay for me to read this?"

"Of course, honey."

Sinking into the rocking chair across from Joan, Sheila opened the envelope, pulled out the letter and began reading. As Joan watched her, she could see the tears welling up in her daughter's eyes. Finally, she lowered the letter to her lap. "That was beautiful, Mom. I could hear Dad's voice in those words. It was so like him—the way he talks. I've always loved that about his letters. He would write just the way he'd say it to you in person."

Joan nodded. "Your father had a way with words. That's for certain."

"Well we will definitely find room in the car for that box of things, or else I will take them to UPS and have them mailed up to my place. I'll discuss it with Rick when he calls tonight, and we'll figure out what's the best way to get them there."

"Okay. Whatever you two decide is fine with me."

Sheila stood and walked over to her, handing her Phil's letter. "Thanks for sharing this with me, Mom." She leaned down and gave her a kiss, and Joan reached around with her good arm and hugged her.

Sheila headed out for the shed to examine the box of gifts and decide the best way to transport them to Sandy Cove. As she pushed open the door of her father's retreat, a flood of memories propelled her back to her childhood. The shed had been her playhouse at one time. She remembered hosting tea parties there with her father's lanky form perched on a child-size chair, his knees nudging the tabletop. In addition, there were teddy bears and dolls joining in the festivities, as Sheila served them their imaginary tea and cookies.

She sank down on her father's stool and sighed. A little girl's aching heart replaced her own as she remembered her father's playful zest for life and his love of surprises. Even now, he was reaching down from heaven with unexpected Christmas gifts for all of them.

Leaning over, she lifted the flaps of the large box in the middle of the floor. There were quite a few awkwardly wrapped packages inside, each labeled with the name of the intended recipient. As she fingered them, she imagined her dad fumbling with the wrapping paper and tape. She could see the grin on his face as he packed them into this box, knowing the surprises and blessings in each hidden treasure.

And then she thought back to the days when she'd been a young mother. The excitement he brought to their home each Christmas as he lavished his grandchildren with homemade gifts and taught them about the birth of Christ.

John had been resistant to that part of their visit, but somehow Sheila had convinced her agnostic husband to allow her father to share his faith with their little ones. How glad she was now. All her father's gentle spiritual input and patient prayers were coming to fruition.

Thank you, Dad, she whispered as she closed the lid of the box. Retrieving a roll of masking tape from his workbench, she began securing the flaps.

Joan's appointment with the doctor went well. He seemed confident the swelling was down enough for a plaster cast. His follow-up x-ray showed a simple fracture, requiring no surgery. "That's the good news," he said. "The bad news is that in people your age, it takes longer for the bone to heal. I'm afraid you are looking at wearing the cast for at least six to eight weeks. If the bone heals well, you'll be able to avoid surgery. Let's schedule an appointment for mid November."

"I'll be in Oregon then," Joan replied. "I probably won't be back to Mariposa until the first of the year."

"Then I'd recommend finding an orthopedic surgeon up there who can monitor your healing process. Where will you be staying?"

"In Sandy Cove."

"Is that near Portland?"

"A little over an hour," Sheila interjected. "But we'd be happy to take her there for a follow-up appointment."

"Great. I know a good orthopedic there. I'll have my nurse give you the information and I can send a copy of her chart and x-rays there electronically."

Once the cast was in place, they headed home.

⟳

Rick arrived the next day, driving a rental van. He looked a little road weary to Joan, but his eyes lit up when he saw Sheila. Joan watched them embrace and felt almost like a voyeur when they kissed each other tenderly.

Turning her gaze away, she thanked God once again for bringing this new man into her daughter's life. Sheila was too young to live the rest of her life as a widow. While Joan knew Phil was the only husband she'd ever hold in her arms, she was equally convinced that this relationship between Sheila and Rick was a blessing from above.

A moment later, she felt Rick's hand on her good shoulder as he bent down and kissed her cheek. "How are you feeling, Joan?" he asked, genuine concern in his voice.

"Better every day," she replied, reaching up and patting his hand.

Sheila cooked the three of them a delicious dinner of pot roast, mashed potatoes, and steamed asparagus. They sat together and visited while they ate, Joan asking Rick about the classes he was currently teaching at the university.

After they'd chatted about his job and Joan's wrist injury, the conversation turned to packing and the trip back to Sandy Cove.

"I'd like to take a look at the things you are planning to take before we decide what to do about the box in the shed," he said. "That's probably some pretty precious cargo, right?"

"Right," Joan replied. "I'd almost rather send some of my winter clothes through the mail and take that box in the rental van with us if we can fit it." She turned to Sheila. "Who knows what your father has hidden inside? I'd hate to have anything break in transit."

"I agree," her daughter said. "We'll take the box, as much of your clothes as we can, and put Thumper in the back seat with you."

Rick wanted to look everything over himself, so he and Sheila headed out to the shed. As they walked down the path, Joan noticed Sheila reach for his hand. He pulled her close and she leaned her head on his shoulder for a moment. Seeing these simple expressions of affection warmed Joan's heart, and she could remember how many times she'd walked the same path just like that with Phil.

When they returned to the house, Rick told her that there would be plenty of room in the van for the box. "Tomorrow morning, Sheila and I will take your extra clothes to UPS and send them off. Then we'll pack up the van and head out."

"I was hoping to go to church on Sunday morning to say goodbye," Joan said.

"Rick's got to get back for his Monday classes, Mom. We really need to leave tomorrow. But I promise we'll do the best we can to get to church up there on Sunday morning."

Although she was disappointed, Joan relented. "I'll call Pastor Lawrence and Catherine this evening," she said.

After the dishes were done, Sheila said, "Rick and I are going to take Thumper for a walk."

Immediately the dog's ears perked up, and he began turning in circles excitedly.

"Guess he heard that," Rick observed with a smile.

Sheila retrieved the leash and clipped it onto Thumper's collar, then the three of them headed out the front door.

"Guess this is as good a time as any to make my phone call," Joan said aloud. Using her left hand, she retrieved her phone book from the end table, propped it open with her cast, and dialed the Taylor's home number.

Pastor Lawrence was almost like family to her. He'd worked under Phil as an assistant pastor before becoming the senior pastor when Phil had to step down from full time ministry. Phil had married Lawrence and Catherine, and Lawrence had presided over Phil's memorial service, sharing a wealth of memories and accolades about the man who'd meant so much to all of them.

The thought of moving away was bittersweet. She knew being near Sheila was important now. And she relished the idea of being able to see her granddaughter and great grandchildren. But her church family...well, that was going to be hard to leave. Once she finally moved for good, she knew she'd likely never see any of them this side of heaven.

Lawrence Taylor was very encouraging about her move. "Being near your daughter will be such a blessing, Joan. I know Phil would want that."

And Catherine, who was on the other phone, said, "We've been hoping to take a road trip up to Washington to see some of my cousins. If we do, we'll be sure to stop in Sandy Cove. Besides, you'll be back to finish packing the house, right?"

"Yes. Probably in January," Joan replied. She paused and then added, "I'll sure miss the Christmas Eve service with all of you."

"We'll miss you, too, Joan," Catherine said. "Both you and Phil."

Lawrence agreed, reflecting, "This will be our first holiday service without him reading the Christmas story in Luke. He will be greatly missed."

Joan flashed back to Phil sitting on a stool on the church stage, his Bible resting in one hand as he shared the account of Jesus' birth. It was something she and the rest of the congregation looked forward to each year, especially after he'd stepped down as their full time minister. The first year, he'd resisted the idea, saying it was Lawrence's place now. But after Lawrence insisted and involved some of the elders in the ceremony as well, Phil's reading from Luke became an annual tradition.

Maybe it's best that I won't be there this year, Joan thought. She cleared her throat. "Lawrence, I'm sure you will do a wonderful job of sharing the account of our Savior's birth this year. You know, Phil was so very proud of you and your ability to effectively share the word of God."

"Thank you, Joan. That means a lot to me," he replied. "Do you need any help with anything before you leave?"

"No. Sheila's friend came down to help us. He's rented a van and will be taking care of loading everything I'm taking."

"How about the house? Is there anything we can do while you are up in Sandy Cove until January?" Catherine asked.

"I'm just going to lock things up here. The neighbor boy will take care of the yard for me."

"Okay. Well, feel free to call us if anything comes up."

"I will," Joan promised. "Thanks again." She paused and then added, "I mean for everything. Your friendship means the world to me."

"We feel the same way, Joan," Lawrence said. "Let's pray before we hang up."

"That would be great. Thanks," Joan replied, hearing a little of her husband in her pastor's voice.

With a calm and steady voice, Pastor Lawrence lifted Joan and her future to the God they loved so much. He prayed for her safety, peace of mind and heart, special family times, and God's best for her future. By the end of his prayer, she felt her heart nestled into God's protective care.

Almost in a whisper, she said, "Thank you. Thank you so very much."

CHAPTER TWELVE

Joan was exhausted by the time they arrived back in Sandy Cove. Even the slightest jostling of the van was uncomfortable with her cast and sling. Twice Thumper had jumped up on her seat to bark at something he saw out the window, and she had bruises and scratches to show for it. Finally, Rick had rigged up some suitcase barriers to keep him back in the third row seat where he belonged.

They'd stopped several times for meals and bathroom breaks, but made the entire nine-hour drive in one day, leaving Mariposa at six in the morning and arriving in Sandy Cove at six that night.

When they got to Sheila's house, Joan headed for the guest room and carefully lowered herself onto the bed. Although she'd dozed a little on and off in the car, she fell fast asleep as soon as her head hit the pillow. Around nine o'clock that night, Sheila came in, offering to help her get changed into her nightgown and asking if she'd like a little snack or a cup of warm milk before going to bed for the night.

Joan felt so groggy that she accepted the help getting undressed. Then she asked for her toiletry bag, brushed her teeth, and climbed back into bed. The next thing she knew, it was morning.

Wandering out to the kitchen, she found Sheila eating breakfast. "How are you feeling this morning?" her daughter asked.

"A little stiff," Joan replied. "But I slept like a log. I think I was in one position all night."

"Must be a little hard to move around with that cast on."

"Yes. Seems like my back is the only comfortable position." Joan walked over to the teakettle and asked, "Is the water hot?"

Sheila joined her at the stove and put her arm around her shoulder. "No. Sorry, Mom. But I did make a fresh pot of coffee. Would you like me to make you some tea?"

"Coffee's fine. Maybe I'll have some tea later on."

Opening the dishwasher, Sheila retrieved a clean cup from the top rack and filled it with hot coffee. "Here," she said, pulling a chair out from the table and setting down the coffee. "Have a seat and I'll make you something to eat."

"I can fix something, dear. You don't need to go to any trouble," Joan replied.

"It's no trouble. And I know it's difficult for you with that cast. Just sit and relax and let me take care of you for a change." Sheila's smile and the tone of her voice communicated the love and patience Joan so desperately needed.

"Thanks, sweetheart." She sank into the chair and took a sip of the delicious brew.

Sheila busied herself toasting some bread and scrambling an egg. When she placed the simple meal before Joan, she felt truly blessed and thankful. "Perfect, honey. Thanks." She bowed her head and silently prayed before beginning her meal.

After she'd finished eating, she suddenly remembered Thumper. "Where's the dog?" she asked.

"Rick took him over to Michelle's last night after he unloaded the van. The old boy seemed happy to see the kids and they were equally excited to have him back."

Joan nodded. "That's good. He's a bit much for me to handle right now."

"They're happy to keep him as long as you want, Mom. For now, you just focus on resting and healing that arm."

"Okay, dear. But I don't want to be a burden to you. I mean it. And don't adjust your plans around me. I know you and Rick have been spending quite a bit of time together, and I don't want my being here to interfere with that. You have your own life to live, and I'll just head right back to Mariposa if I see that you are hovering over me and ignoring him."

Sheila laughed. "I promise not to hover. And you're not a burden. I love having you here. Really. So get that idea out of your head."

They chatted some more about the week ahead, and then decided to get ready for the day. "Let me help you get unpacked and dressed," Sheila said, following her into the guest room.

Joan hated to have to rely on someone else to help dress her, but the truth was that having her right arm immobilized in the cast and sling made it next to impossible to do it on her own. And hanging up clothes? Well that was out of the question. "I'm sorry to be such a gimp," she said.

"Stop apologizing, Mom. I'm glad to help." Sheila quickly made up the bed, placed Joan's suitcase on it, and began unpacking. "What would you like to wear today?" she asked as she started carrying clothes into the closet.

Joan pointed out some clothes, and Sheila helped her change into them. "Maybe tonight you can help me with a little sponge bath before bed," Joan said.

"I'd be happy to. You just let me know what you need, okay?" she replied, gently giving her a hug. "I'm going to the market this morning after I get dressed, so make a list of whatever you need or want."

After Sheila left the room, Joan sank down onto the bed and prayed. *Thank You, Lord, for our sweet, sweet daughter and for how much she helps me. Please don't let me become a burden to her. Help my arm to heal quickly so that I can take care of myself. And, Lord, would you please tell Phil I love him and miss him?*

She stood up, walked into the bathroom, and began the task of brushing her teeth and hair with her left hand.

The days melted into weeks, and the weeks blended into each other as Joan rested and healed. She enjoyed Sheila's company and felt much less lonely than she had in Mariposa.

She learned to navigate life with a cast and sling, and tried her best not to make demands on her daughter's time, relishing the love she could see developing and blossoming between Sheila and Rick. The joy on her daughter's face almost made up for the sorrow in her own heart over the loss of her precious Phil.

But she still thought of him numerous times throughout each day, and missed his cheerful countenance, his confident faith, and his zest for life. It seemed as if a decade of extra years had been added to her age by his absence. Although she'd marveled at the idea of being great grandparents when they'd shared that role together, now she truly felt the part.

"Grief is a funny thing," she said one day as she and her granddaughter, Michelle, were enjoying a cup of tea together after a long day. "It hits like huge waves in the sea, one after the other, at first. Then the waves are a little less frequent until eventually a whole day may pass without one hitting. But when it does, each wave is nearly as intense as the first. And they can come at the most unexpected times."

"You're right. I'd never thought of it that way," Michelle replied. "But that's how I felt after Dad died. And now I feel the same since Grandpa passed away."

Joan looked at her and felt such love and gratitude for a young, busy mother and teacher, who would make time for an old lady like her. "You are such a treasure to me," she said, reaching out and squeezing Michelle's hand.

"I love you, Grandma. And I'm so very glad you chose to come live in Sandy Cove."

Joan thought about what she'd seen of the Shoreline Manor complex. It wasn't her home in Mariposa. That was certain. But the grounds looked well kept and attractive, and the apartments were modern and in relatively new condition. Somehow she'd find a way to feel at home there. She must. Now that she'd spent the past couple of months here, she knew she needed to be close to family. There was no going back to Mariposa.

Sheila and Rick offered to go back there after Christmas. They would sort through the things Joan hadn't gotten around to before her fall. They even offered to host an estate sale for the extra furniture and household items she wouldn't need or be able to use in her new place.

Joan was reluctant to sell the house, so they decided to have the church help them find a family to rent it for a year or two. It seemed like the perfect solution, and she really hoped the renters would be a young family who would enjoy the property and build some of their own memories, just like she and Phil had as they brought up their daughter.

"Oh, Phil," she said one night, as she was getting ready for bed, "I sure am going to miss you during the holidays. Sometimes I look up at the clouds and wonder if you really are there, in that great cloud of witnesses, cheering me on." She smiled and sighed, then climbed into bed and hugged his pillow in her arms, a practice she'd begun when he'd been in the hospital bed in the front room. It was one of the things that helped her feel close to him even now.

93

Thanksgiving was rushing up in only one more week. And then Christmas. Her first Christmas without Phil.

CHAPTER THIRTEEN

Sheila and Rick had just returned from an evening out doing some early Christmas shopping. Joan was asleep in her room, so they sat quietly in the living room enjoying just being alone together.

"I've been thinking about your father," Rick said, his arm draped over her shoulder as his fingertips caressed her shoulder.

"Really? Me, too."

"Remember what Pastor Ben said at his memorial service?"

She turned to look at him. "Which part?"

"About living life fully with no regrets, and the importance of realizing that none of us is guaranteed tomorrow."

She nodded. "Yeah. So true."

He shifted his body, pulling his arm away and turning to face her. Then he took her hands in his. "I really care about you, Sheila."

"I care about you, too," she replied.

He looked her in the eye and added, "What I'm trying to say is that I've fallen in love with you. And I don't want us to miss any of whatever time we might have."

She studied his face.

"I know we haven't been dating that long, but I can't imagine ever feeling this way about anyone else. In all my years as a bachelor," he paused and gazed at her for a moment, "I never thought I'd ever find someone like you."

"Oh, Rick," Sheila began. But he put his finger over her lips.

"Let me finish," he said. Clearing his throat, he continued. "Although I'm not the man your father was, I'd like the chance to make the rest of your life happy and fulfilling. If you'll let me, that is."

She studied his face. "Dr. Chambers, are you proposing to me?" she asked, her heart racing.

Looking down at their interlaced fingers and then back up into her eyes, he replied, "Let's just say, hypothetically speaking, that I am. Proposing, I mean. What would your answer be?"

She leaned over and kissed him, an unmistakable love communicated without words. "I think you'd have a pretty good chance," she said.

His lips found hers again, and their kiss stirred profound tenderness and passion. "Be my wife, Sheila Ackerman," he whispered.

"It would be my pleasure," she replied, her voice thick with emotion.

Thanksgiving arrived with a blustery, cool, but surprisingly clear day. After several weeks of rain, the sunshine and blue skies were a welcome relief. To top it off, Joan's cast was removed the week before and she was thoroughly enjoying being able to use her right arm and hand again.

Michelle was hosting the Thanksgiving family celebration, and all were invited, including their good friends, Pastor Ben Johnson, Ben's wife Kelly, and their five children—Luke, Lucy, Logan, and the twins, Liam and Lily. Even Michelle's brother, Tim, and his girlfriend, Traci were making the trek up from Southern California to join the gathering. And, of course, Sheila's beau, Rick, said he wouldn't miss the big day.

Joan had offered to make her traditional yam casserole and pumpkin pies, so she was up early, working busily in the kitchen.

"Those pies smell delicious," Sheila said, as she came in to fix some breakfast. "You always were the queen of desserts, Mom. Especially the holiday pies."

Joan smiled as she lifted the second one from the oven and placed it on a rack on the counter. "Your father would sit in the kitchen all day, hoping for a chance to snag a slice. 'I just want to give it the taste test,' he'd say."

"Yeah. Dad was always big on sweets," Sheila replied, and then added, "Anything I can help with?"

"You can open the cans of yams and drain them if you'd like. But maybe you want to eat something yourself, first. I left some oatmeal on the stove for you."

"You've really been cooking up a storm, Mom." She lifted the lid of the pan and scooped some oatmeal into a bowl. "From scratch, as usual," she observed.

"Is there any other way?" Joan replied with a wink. "Those instant packets are for the birds. This will put some meat on your bones."

Sheila laughed. "I don't really want any more meat on them," she said, patting her hip. "There's plenty of padding here to last a lifetime."

"Nonsense. You've still got a cute figure. I've seen how that man of yours looks at you," Joan said as she pulled a quart of milk out of the fridge and handed it to her daughter. "Want some nuts and berries on that?"

"No thanks. Better save my calories for the feast."

After eating her oatmeal, Sheila began working by her side, helping to mash the yams, add the marshmallows and brown sugar, pat the mixture into balls, and roll them in cornflake crumbs before placing them into the baking pan.

As the two ladies chatted about past Thanksgivings, Joan noticed a special sparkle in her daughter's eyes. And she found a little thankful joy creeping into her heart.

Rick picked them up at two o'clock, and soon the ladies were busy in the kitchen with Michelle and Kelly as the men retreated to the family room to watch football. Tim and Traci pulled in an hour later, and Michelle welcomed Traci into the female proceedings while Tim collapsed on the floor in front of the television.

Michelle and Steve's son, Caleb, and Ben and Kelly's son, Logan, and their twins were enjoying the sunny day out in the back yard. Caleb had his remote control car racing around the patio with Logan's. Luke, age fourteen, was part of the male bonding group in the family room, while Lucy helped Michelle and Steve's daughter, Madison, decorate and set the tables and put out the name cards.

Joan loved being surrounded by family and friends. But she also felt a little out of place without Phil trailing her around and sneaking bites or contributing to the banter about the game. With so many young people gathered together, it was easy to feel old.

"Are you okay, Grandma?" Michelle asked, draping her arm over her shoulder.

Joan looked up into her granddaughter's eyes and smiled. "Sure, honey. Just feeling my age a little." As Madison came into the kitchen for the silverware, Joan flashed back to another Thanksgiving, many years back, when Sheila had been that age. Both Joan and Phil's parents had come for the holiday, and she'd been so nervous cooking for all of them.

"Relax, sweetheart," Phil had said. "Everything you touch in the kitchen turns into a culinary delight."

"Oh, pshaw," she'd replied, as she scooted him out of the room to go visit. But his confidence had rubbed off on her, and she'd been able to enjoy what would have otherwise been a very stressful evening.

"Penny for your thoughts," Sheila said, pulling Joan back to the moment.

"You sound just like your father," she replied, giving Sheila's cheek a little pinch. "I was just taking a quick stroll down memory lane. But I'm back now, so let's finish up in here and help Michelle serve this feast."

As they all sat down around the table, Steve reached out his hands, just like Phil used to do, and they formed a connected circle. "Ben, would you ask a blessing on the food?"

"I'd be honored." As they bowed their heads, Ben thanked God for each person present and for the delicious food they were about to eat. "And we ask, Lord, that You would give Phil a hug for us and tell him how much we all miss him."

Joan looked up, tears of gratitude glistening in her eyes. Clearly, she was not the only one thinking about her dear husband tonight.

The food was scrumptious, and she found herself eating more than she had in quite a while. After they all stuffed themselves, Michelle passed around a basket with slips of paper and pencils. She instructed them to write something they were thankful for, sign their names, and put the papers back in the same basket.

"I'm going to save these papers, roll them up like tiny scrolls and tie red and green ribbons around them. They'll help decorate our Christmas tree, and then I'll keep them in a safe place until next Thanksgiving when I'll give them back to you," she said.

Everyone went to work, including the children. Kelly suggested the twins draw a picture of what they were thankful for, and they busily went to work. Other than

Caleb asking Logan how to spell a few words, the room was quiet as pencils scratched out a myriad of blessings.

Next, Michelle asked them to each share what they had written. One by one, they stood and revealed what they were most thankful for. Afterward, she turned to Joan and said, "Grandma, would you do us the honor of praying a short prayer of thanks for these many blessings? Yours and Grandpa's examples of gratefulness have provided such a special legacy for us."

Joan was moved to tears. She carefully stood to her feet, using the table to help support her trembling legs. As she freely allowed her tears to flow, she prayed a heartfelt prayer of thanksgiving for the many ways God had blessed and provided for her loved ones gathered here. By the end, many others seated at the table had their hearts stirred, and Joan noticed some other eyes that were no longer dry.

They were all about to get up and go into the living room, when Sheila stopped them. Clearing her throat, she reached her left hand under the table to Rick, who'd pulled something out of his pocket. Then she said, "Rick and I have a little announcement to make."

Joan instantly knew. But she said nothing as her heart rose into her throat one more time.

Sheila glanced lovingly over at Rick.

"What Sheila's trying to say," he began, "is that she's accepted my request to become my wife."

Joan's daughter pulled her hand out from under the table and held it up for all to see. A beautiful platinum and diamond ring rested securely on her finger.

Joy swept over Joan as she gazed at her daughter's radiant smile. "This is the best news of the evening," she said. And everyone agreed.

That night as she got into bed, Joan reached over and picked up the brochure for Shoreline Manor on the nightstand. "I have a feeling I'll be moving here soon," she said to herself, as she looked at the pictures again before turning out the light.

CHAPTER FOURTEEN

The next few weeks were a flurry of events as wedding plans competed with Christmas shopping, gift wrapping, and decorating Sheila's house. Joan knew Sheila had her hands full, and she hated to add to the demands on her daughter's time, but she really wanted to do some Christmas shopping herself.

"Would you mind taking me out for a couple of hours this afternoon?" she asked one morning.

"Of course not, Mom. Where would you like to go?"

"To a few little shops in town. I want to look for some gifts."

Sheila smiled at her. "You know you don't need to buy any Christmas gifts, right? Just having you with us is a gift itself."

"Nonsense. I have a little money put aside for this, and I'd order things through my catalogs, but I'm just not sure they would get here in time."

"Okay. Well let's make an afternoon of it. I've been wanting to discuss the wedding with you anyway. We could go out to lunch, and then run your errands."

"Thanks, dear. That sounds great." Joan's spirits lifted as she thought about a lunch date with her daughter. And maybe planning a wedding would be just what she needed to get her mind off of Phil.

A new teahouse had opened in town, and it was decked out for Christmas with beautiful white lights, poinsettias, and a variety of small pine trees with old-fashioned ornaments and garlands. "This will be my treat," Sheila told her as they took their seats in a cozy corner by the fireplace. After ordering some pumpkin soup, tea sandwiches, and scones, they sat back and sipped their cinnamon-flavored brew. The sound of string instruments playing Christmas tunes in the background combined with the crackling fire to create a cozy atmosphere for their midday meal.

"This is lovely, Sheila. I'm glad you discovered this place," she said to her daughter.

"I'm glad you like it. I've been wanting to give it a try since it opened last month," she replied.

"So tell me about your wedding plans. Have you set a date?"

"Well, actually, yes. We have," Sheila began. "You remember the message by Ben at Dad's memorial service—about living life to the fullest don't you?"

Joan nodded. Images of Phil raced into her mind as she recalled him also talking about that when he'd told her he didn't want to spend the last few weeks or months of his life steeped in chemotherapy. Forcing her attention back to her daughter, she said, "Your father always felt that way, too."

Sheila reached over and squeezed her hand as if realizing how difficult this time must be for her. "Ben's message really impacted Rick and me, Mom. We want to get married soon, and we've decided New Year's Eve would be a great anniversary to celebrate together each year."

Joan tried to imagine what it must be like for her daughter to be so in love at this later stage of life. "I think that's a wonderful idea, dear. I'm so very happy for you two."

"We're thinking a simple ceremony conducted by Ben at the Chapel by the Sea. It would be a family-only event with a dinner reception at the Cliffhanger Restaurant."

"How can I help?" Joan asked.

"There really isn't anything I can think of right now."

"Well, at least let me buy you a new dress for the occasion."

Sheila smiled. "That's very generous of you, Mom. But I was thinking I could wear the dress I wore to Michelle's wedding. It still fits and I've never had an opportunity to wear anything that dressy since then."

Joan nodded. "May I pay for the dinner reception, then?"

"Absolutely not. Rick wants to cover that." Then, as if she could read Joan's mind, Sheila added, "Your love and support are the greatest gifts you could ever give me, Mom. I mean that."

"Okay, dear. I just wish there was *something* I could contribute to this special event." Joan remembered how much she'd done for Sheila's first wedding, and what a blessing it was to help her daughter plan and prepare for the big day. Now she felt more like an invited guest than the mother of the bride.

"There is one thing you could do, Mom," her daughter said.

"What's that?"

"You could say the prayer before our reception dinner. That would mean so much to both Rick and to me."

Joan could hear the unspoken words of her daughter's request. This would have been something Phil would have been asked to do. "I'd be honored, Sheila," she replied, fighting back emotions that threatened to invade their lovely lunch together.

After they'd eaten, Joan got up the nerve to ask, "What about my move to Shoreline Manor?"

"There's no hurry, Mom," she said with a reassuring smile. "In fact, Rick is fine having you stay on with us if you'd like."

"Absolutely not, Sheila. You two need your privacy. And I'm itching to get into a place of my own," she added, hoping she sounded convincing. "Let's give them a call when we get home today."

"Whatever you say," her daughter replied.

Their shopping adventure was productive, and soon they were headed home with parcels of gifts in tow. After they unloaded the car and changed into some comfortable casual wear for the evening, Joan retrieved the brochure for Shoreline Manor from her bedroom.

"I'll call them, Mom," Sheila offered.

"Okay. Just set up an appointment for this week or next."

A week later, Joan and Sheila were headed over for another tour of the senior apartment complex at Shoreline Manor.

As soon as they got out of the car, Joan's stomach began to feel queasy and her heart fluttered. She'd never made a big move like this without Phil, and it seemed intimidating and a bit scary. What if she moved here and then wasn't happy? How would it feel to be surrounded by old people all day every day? And what would it be like to be alone every night?

On the other hand, she knew she couldn't stay at Sheila's house. It just wouldn't be fair to her daughter and new son-in-law. No matter how much they tried to reassure her she was welcome there, she knew she needed to move.

Dear God, please give me strength to do this, she prayed silently as they walked around the grounds in the shadow of the dark rainclouds overhead.

"Mom? Are you okay?" her daughter asked. "You seem kind of quiet."

"I'm fine," Joan said, forcing a smile.

"You know you don't have to make any decisions right now. We can wait until after the holidays."

Their tour guide cleared her throat. "I don't mean to be pushy here, but there are several other people looking at the available units. I'd recommend deciding as soon as possible if you think you are interested."

Joan nodded. "Yes. I think that is a good idea. Let's just continue our tour. Hopefully we'll finish before the rain."

After walking around the entire complex and seeing the apartments, the dining hall, the recreation room, the vegetable garden, and a couple of the available apartments, Joan made her decision. She'd take one of the downstairs units facing the courtyard with its beautiful landscaping and fountains. The contract was drawn up to begin January fifteenth.

That night, Joan couldn't sleep. She kept replaying the tour and her decision to sign a contract. On the way home, she'd found out that Sheila and Rick were planning a honeymoon in Southern California, hoping for a little sunshine in the midst of a wet Oregon winter.

"We could stop in Mariposa on our way south and arrange for movers to finish packing your household items and deliver everything to Shoreline Manor."

"I've boxed up a lot of things that can be donated to the church thrift store," Joan told her.

"Okay, we'll take care of that, too. Rick needs to be back in town on the eighth, so we'll be back just in time to meet the movers and help you get moved in the following week," Sheila added reassuringly.

Christmas morning found a wave of melancholy washing over Joan as she arose from a restless night's sleep. Each new holiday was a challenge in the battle to find joy without Phil. The last thing Joan wanted to do was to put a damper on everyone's holiday. *Please help me, Father. I need Your strength and grace today.*

She thought about the box she'd found in the shed. Today she'd finally get to see what Phil had been working on those last few weeks of his life. She had mixed feelings about opening it. Something about having it there unopened gave the feeling Phil's life wasn't quite completely over. A part of him was in that box, awaiting discovery. She figured it was probably a couple of things for the kids.

She never would have imagined the treasures that her beloved husband had tucked into that package.

"Mom, are you almost ready?" Sheila asked through her bedroom door. "Michelle is expecting us for breakfast in twenty minutes, and you know how impatient the kids get on Christmas morning. I'd hate to keep them waiting."

"Just give me a minute, honey," Joan replied, silently chiding herself for taking so much time to get moving and get dressed.

A few minutes later, she tracked down Sheila in the front room, pulling gifts out from under the tree to put in the car. "Did you get the box?" Joan asked.

Sheila looked up at her from the floor. "Box?"

"The one your father put together before..." Her voice faltered.

"Oh. Yes, it's already in the back. Rick loaded it in for me last night before he left."

Joan nodded. She looked away to regain her composure. After a deep breath and another quick silent prayer, she asked if Sheila needed any help with the gifts.

"No. This is the last of them," her daughter said, standing to her feet with a couple of brightly wrapped boxes in her arms and several gift bags dangling from her wrist. "Are you ready?"

"Yeah, I guess." Joan replied, trying to sound cheerful.

Sheila paused. "I know this is going to be hard for you, Mom. Without Dad, I mean."

"Now don't you go worrying about me." Joan forced a smile as she reached out and squeezed her daughter's arm. "I miss your father something fierce, but it's a blessing to be here with you and Michelle and the kids." She paused and then added, "Just think. Next year at this time, you will be celebrating Christmas as Rick's wife."

Nodding and smiling, Sheila said, "And we will want you right there with us."

Michelle had created a lovely spread for their breakfast. Piping hot bacon and egg casserole, blueberry and bran muffins, and fresh fruit were set up in the center of the table. Caleb was nosing around under the tree, pulling out his presents and stacking them in one pile, as Madison helped her mother pour the juice and water.

"Caleb, come on in here and let's eat," Michelle called from the dining room as the rest of the family took their seats.

After a moment of silence, Steve stood up. "I'll go get him."

They could hear his voice as he said, "Come on, sport. The sooner we eat, the sooner we can get to the gifts."

"Okay, Dad," Caleb's reluctant voice responded. They rounded the corner and sat down.

As was the family's tradition, Steve opened his Bible to the passage in Luke about the birth of Christ. Everyone listened attentively as he read it aloud, pausing a couple of times to ask the kids questions like, "And what was the name of the angel?" or "What is impossible with God?"

Joan enjoyed seeing their responsive faces and Steve's animated gestures as he read. *These kids are getting a gift that is so much more precious than those under the tree,* she thought.

Finally, it was time to thank God for the meal. "Caleb, would you pray for us today?" Steve asked.

"Sure, Dad," the little boy replied. "Dear Jesus, thank you for your birthday and for letting us get presents even though it's really not our day. Thank you for Mommy and Daddy and Madison and Uncle Tim and Grandma and Dr. Chambers and Great Grandma and Thumper. And for this food. Amen."

"Amen," everyone replied in unison.

As they started passing around the food, Joan couldn't help but wonder if Caleb would remember his great grandfather when he grew up. She knew that he'd been sneaking looks around the table as he prayed because he named everyone in the order in which they were seated. It was natural that he wouldn't include Phil in his prayer. But it did cause her to reflect on the very real possibility that he would eventually forget him completely.

She tried to remain upbeat and enjoy the wonderful meal Michelle had prepared. Much of the adult conversation revolved around Rick and Sheila's wedding plans, and she could see Caleb's impatience as people finished eating and continued to visit over coffee.

"Dad," he said with a bit of a whine in his voice. "Is it almost time now?"

Steve reached over and ruffled his son's hair. "Almost. Why don't you go out back and give Thumper his present," he suggested.

"Okay!" Caleb jumped up and ran back into the living room, then passed by them again with a large rawhide bone in his hand.

"Looks like your son decided to open Thumper's present for him," Michelle observed, winking at Steve.

They heard the back door slap against the jamb as Caleb took the bone outside.

Sheila pushed out her chair and started collecting dishes to carry to the kitchen. Almost immediately, Rick was on his feet assisting.

"You two don't need to do that," Michelle said, standing up and grabbing some dishes herself.

"Nonsense," Sheila said. "We're happy to help."

Soon all the adults were carrying plates and serving dishes into the kitchen, as Madison helped with the glasses and cups.

"Thanks, everyone," Michelle said, as she put the extra food away.

"Why don't the rest of you go into the living room," Sheila suggested. "Rick and I will rinse the dishes and put them into the dishwasher. We'll be there in a flash."

Joan watched glances exchange between her daughter and granddaughter. *Sometimes those two look like they have telepathy,* she thought.

Then Michelle turned and ushered everyone out of the kitchen, getting them settled around the tree. Presents filled the area surrounding it, and Joan noticed the box from Phil nestled in a back corner.

A moment later, Caleb came bounding into the room, plopping down on the floor beside his stash of gifts.

"Maddie, would you like to hand out the presents?" Michelle asked.

"Sure, Mom." She stood to her feet and walked around the tree, carefully reading package labels and giving each person in the room a gift. "Where's Grandma?" she asked. "She and Dr. Chambers are in the kitchen. They'll be here in a few minutes. You can just put their gifts over here," Michelle said, gesturing to the two vacant seats next to Joan on the couch.

"Here's one for Traci," Madison said, holding up a package from Sheila.

"Just leave that under the tree," Tim replied. "We can give it to her next week when she comes for the wedding."

"Where is Traci?" Caleb asked.

"She's with her family," Tim said. "Remember, we told you at Thanksgiving that she wouldn't be able to come back for Christmas? But she's planning to come for your grandma's wedding, so you'll see her then."

"Oh. Okay," he replied. "Can we start opening our stuff?"

"Let me check on Grandma. I'll be right back," Michelle said. She disappeared for a minute and then returned with her mother and Rick. "Okay. All set!"

Soon ribbons and papers were strewn around the room as gift after gift were opened and shared.

Michelle opened the first of the gifts from Joan. As she carefully removed the wrapping and opened the box, Joan watched for her reaction. Parting the tissue, Michelle lifted the hand-knitted sweater from within. Lavender, charcoal and cream yarns made a beautiful design that created a buzz across the room.

"Did you make this, Grandma?" Michelle asked as she held up the sweater.

Joan nodded. "I did. And I thought of you with every stitch."

Michelle's eyes filled with tears. "I absolutely love it," she said.

"Can I see it, Mom?" Maddie asked.

Handing it to her, Michelle said, "Pass it around for everyone to see."

The next gift from Joan went to Sheila. It was a tiny box wrapped in gold foil paper. "Mom?" Sheila asked.

"It's something my mother gave me before my wedding, honey. She'd worn it in hers, and I wore it in mine," Joan explained.

Sheila looked surprised and very curious as she unwrapped the small package. Flipping open the lid, she said in a whisper, "It's beautiful, Mom." She lifted out of the box a delicate gold chain with a tiny gold cross.

"I almost gave it to you before you married John, but before I could do that, you'd already selected a pearl necklace for your wedding," Joan explained.

"It wouldn't have meant the same thing to me then that it does now, Mom. I'm glad you saved it." She turned to Rick and held it up for him to see. "I'll wear it for our wedding."

He smiled and nodded. "Good choice."

Next, Maddie opened Joan's gift for her. "What is this?" she asked as she lifted an album out of the shiny red gift bag.

"It's a scrapbook I made during high school. I thought it might be fun for you to see what my life was like during that time since you are going to be there soon."

All eyes were on Madison as she began paging through the fabric-covered book. "This is really cool. Thanks, Grandma Joan. I love it."

"Let me see," Michelle said when her daughter was finished turning the pages. Caleb walked over and stood by her, looking over her shoulder as they viewed the scrapbook together.

"What are those?" he asked, pointing to slips of papers with names on them.

"Those are my dance cards," Joan replied with a smile. "When we had school dances, the boys would ask if they could be on our dance card. That meant we were promising them a dance."

Caleb nodded, still looking a little confused. "Oh," he replied, evoking some laughs from others in the room.

"What?" he asked.

"Nothing, sport," Steve said, pulling his son onto his lap. "It's just girl stuff."

"Did you bring me something?" the boy asked Joan.

"I sure did," she replied. "It's something that used to belong to your great grandfather when he was a boy." She gestured to a box with red and green plaid paper. "Would you hand that to Caleb, please?" she asked Rick.

Caleb immediately tore into the paper and threw the lid off the box. "Cool! A baseball bat made of wood."

"Your Great Grandpa Phil was quite a baseball player in his time," Joan said. "He could hit the ball out of the park, and everyone in the high school stands would cheer when he came up to bat."

"Really, Mom? I don't remember him talking much about playing baseball," Sheila replied.

"He probably didn't think you'd be interested, honey. But you must remember him playing some Saturdays with the men from church."

"Oh yeah. Now that you mention it, I do remember sitting in the bleachers watching them sometimes," she replied.

Joan smiled and nodded. Then she turned to Tim. "I wasn't sure what to give you, young man. But I thought this might bring back some memories." She bent over to reach for a small package tucked under the tree.

"I'll get it, Grandma Joan," Madison said, reaching down and retrieving it. "Here, Uncle Tim."

Tim opened the box and lifted out a well-worn knife.

"Do you remember learning how to whittle with your grandfather?"

He grinned, his expression reminding her of the little boy who used to sit beside Phil on the porch steps as they carved toys and figures together. "I sure do, Grandma."

"Can I see it?" Caleb piped up.

"Sure, bud. Just be careful." Tim handed him the knife, showing him how to hold it safely.

Once Caleb was finished examining Tim's gift, he asked, "Would you teach me how to widdle?"

"That's *whittle*," Tim replied. "And yes, I'd be happy to teach you. If it's okay with your mom and dad, that is."

"Can he, Dad?" Caleb asked earnestly.

"Sure. He can teach both of us," Steve replied with a nod.

"Well we'd better get on to the rest of these gifts if we want to finish today," Michelle said. "Maddie, why don't you give each person a package to open together?"

Immediately, Madison began distributing the packages. One round of gifts after another were opened, shared, and appreciated around the room, as wrapping paper, ribbons, and gift bags piled up all over the floor.

Finally, Michelle stood and gathered up the mess, cramming the torn paper and discarded ribbons into plastic trash bags.

"Are we all finished?" Madison asked, glancing down at her cell phone.

"Not quite," Rick replied. He and Sheila stood up. "We'll be right back," he said.

They disappeared into the kitchen again, and returned with a box that had holes in the side. He placed it beside Joan on the couch and the box began to move.

"What on earth?" Joan said, looking up into their eyes.

"Go ahead and open it, Mom," Sheila replied with a smile.

As she lifted the lid, a tiny white kitten with blue eyes peered up at her. Joan's heart caught in her throat as she gazed at the puff of fur, which had now begun to meow in

115

a squeaky little voice. Instantly the kids were hovering over the box.

"Oh, she is so adorable!" Maddie exclaimed.

"Can I hold her?" Caleb asked.

"Let's let your great grandma hold her first," Steve said, coming over and gently guiding the kids to back off a bit.

Joan reached down into the box and carefully lifted out the kitten. Cradling the white ball of fur to her chest, she stroked the kitten's head with her chin. A loud purring emanated from the tiny creature.

"Looks like she likes you, Mom," Sheila said, leaning against Rick whose arm was draped over her shoulder.

Joan looked up at her daughter and future son-in-law. "So this is what you've been planning behind my back?" she asked. "I had a feeling you two were up to something when it took you so long to rinse those dishes."

"We had the kitten in the garage. Steve picked her up for us yesterday," Sheila explained.

"Thank you so much, sweetheart. I love her." Joan said happily, reminiscing about all the times she'd been tempted to get a cat but had denied herself because of Phil's allergy to the critters.

Sheila looked up at Rick. "Thank him," she said. "It was his idea."

"Really?" Joan asked, looking into Rick's eyes.

"Sheila mentioned that you'd always wanted a cat. I thought it might be a good time," he said.

Soon the kitten was being passed from person to person as they all discussed names. "I think I'll call her Josie," Joan announced. "I had a best friend growing up named Josie and she had almost white blonde hair like this with the brightest blue eyes."

"Josie suits her," Michelle said as she nuzzled the kitten.

"I agree," Maddie added.

"Then it's decided," Sheila said. "Joan and Josie—it has a nice ring to it," she added with a smile.

"We've got one more thing to open," Madison announced as she dragged the box from Phil out of the corner.

CHAPTER FIFTEEN

The first thing out of the big box from Phil was a package for Caleb. All eyes focused on him as he tore open the wrapping paper. "Red! My favorite color!" he said, lifting out a balsa wood airplane.

"That's the kind of plane I used to have as a kid," Rick said from across the room. "Can I have a look?"

"Sure," Caleb replied, making engine noises as he flew the plane over to him.

"Look here, son," Rick said as he pointed out some lettering on the side.

Caleb pointed and said, "Hey, that's my name."

"Yep. Caleb's Cargo Carrier. Looks like you've got a new business!"

"Let me see it, dear," Joan said, reaching in Caleb's direction.

Holding the plane high above his head, he flew the plane over and gently landed it in her lap. She handed Josie to Sheila and carefully examined the plane. As she ran her fingers over the smooth wood, she imagined Phil sitting out in the shed assembling and painting the aircraft.

"I think there's more," Steve said to Caleb as he lifted another package with the boy's name on it out of the box.

Caleb opened it to discover a children's picture Bible with a bookmark shaped like a sword. "Cool!" he said as he flashed the miniature sword.

"Maybe we can start reading this tonight at bedtime," Steve suggested.

"Good idea, Pops!" the boy replied, and Joan couldn't help but chuckle.

The next present in the big box had Madison's name on it. Quite the opposite of Caleb, she carefully slipped her fingers under the tape and eased the paper off. Inside was a carved wooden box with a heart on top engraved with the letter M. As she lifted the lid, she discovered a dainty gold cross necklace and a white leather Bible with her name in gold letters in the bottom right cover of the front.

As she held up the Bible to show everyone, Michelle turned to Joan and said, "That's just like the Bible you and Grandpa gave me when I was Maddie's age."

Madison took her items over and showed them to Joan, one by one. Then she leaned over and hugged her great grandma. "Thank you, Grandma Joan. I love them."

As she admired the handiwork on the box, she replied, "Don't thank me, sweetheart. These were from your Grandpa Phil. He did this all on his own."

Madison snuggled up against her. "I miss Grandpa," she said sadly.

"Me, too, honey," Joan replied, tipping her head and leaning it against her great granddaughter's.

Just then, Sheila squealed. "I guess we'd better get this little kitty into the litter box," she said, holding the dripping feline in one hand as she cupped the other under it's bottom. "I'll be right back."

Rick leapt to his feet and followed her, opening the door into the garage so she could continue to hold Josie securely.

Soon they returned to the festivities. "Let's see what else Dad packed in there," Sheila said as she and Rick took their seats.

Next out of the box was a gift for Michelle. In similar fashion to her daughter, she delicately unwrapped the package slowly.

"Just rip it!" Caleb exclaimed, and everyone laughed.

Michelle lifted out a hand mirror with an intricately carved frame. Attached to it was a little note ~ *When you look into this mirror, Princess, remember that the young lady you see in that reflection is the Daughter of a King and the Bride of Christ.* She walked over to Joan and perched on the arm of the couch beside her. "Look, Grandma. Isn't it beautiful?"

Joan took the mirror in her hands and inspected the craftsmanship of the floral vine that wrapped around the glass. Running her fingers over the raised flowers, she imagined Phil doing his own final inspection. It was almost as if she could feel the impression of his fingertips on the wood.

"Do you think he actually carved this himself?" Michelle asked.

"I'm certain of it, honey. Your grandfather carved a mirror for me for our first Christmas together. It wasn't nearly this detailed. But over the years, he got lots of practice whittling away back there in that shed."

"I'll treasure it forever," her granddaughter said as Joan handed it back to her.

A box with Tim's name on it was the next package out of the box. Inside was an old black Bible with Timothy engraved on the front. He flipped it open to find an envelope inside. Pulling out the letter inside, he began to read silently while everyone watched.

"Read it out loud," Caleb said, leaning against his uncle.

"Okay, here goes." Tim cleared his throat and began. "Dear Tim, This Bible was my grandfather's. His name was Timothy, too. It seemed fitting that you should have it. He spent a lot of time with this book, and I still remember sitting under the old sycamore tree at his house, as he'd read passages aloud to me. His love for scripture was what motivated mine.

"You've got a godly heritage, young man. I sure do hope you'll follow in the footsteps of my Grandpa Tim, and sink your roots deep into the heart of God. No matter how carefree and easygoing your life may be today, we all have our share of challenges along life's path. The words you find in these pages are so much more than just words. They are life and hope and a promise for tomorrow. Don't miss those treasures, Tim. They are for you.

"I've left one more item for you, too. But it wouldn't fit in this box. You'll find it out in the corner of my garage with a red blanket covering it. Remember that wagon we built together when you were seven or eight years old? Well, I did a little work on that project of ours, and it's up and running again and ready to use. You're an uncle now, and hopefully one day you'll also be a dad. That wagon is for you to share with the kids in your life. Take good care of her. She's looking pretty good now.

"I'll be waiting for you on the other side, son, and I'll be looking forward to hearing all your adventures. Love, Grandpa." Tim's voice cracked a little as he read the last line. When he looked up, his eyes met Joan's, and she could see his tears.

"Come over here, honey," she said.

Tim came and knelt in front of her and she wrapped her arms around him as they both dissolved into tears. The room was silent and everyone was still. Finally, Tim pulled back a little and gave her a kiss on the cheek. "I'll never forget him, Grandma. Promise."

She couldn't speak. But she nodded and tried to give him the best smile she had as she wiped away the tears.

No one moved except Tim, who turned and sat at Joan's feet leaning against the couch for support. Michelle reached down and put her hand on her brother's shoulder for a moment, and he turned, looked up at her and smiled.

Finally, Joan said, "Is there anything else in there?"
Steve peered into the box. "Oh. There's something
here for me," he said, sounding surprised.

"Open it, Dad," Caleb piped up.

"It's another Bible," Steve said as he opened the
package.

"That one was Phil's," Joan said, instantly recognizing
the worn leather cover. "It was his first Bible when he
started preaching."

Steve opened it to find his own letter in the front. As
he pulled the stationery out of the envelope, something
gold fell to the floor at his feet. He stooped down and
picked up a girl's ring with a tiny diamond.

"What does the letter say, honey?" Michelle asked.

Steve skimmed through it and handed it to her. As she
read it, her eyes teared up.

"Read it to us, Mom," Caleb requested.

"This one's not a read aloud, sweetheart," she said.
Then she handed it to her mother, who read through it and
passed it on to Joan.

Joan lifted the paper and began to read silently.

Dear Steve,

*This ring is like the one I gave to our daughter when she was
Madison's age. I wanted her to know how very special she was to me,
and that she was also a treasure to God.*

*It's tough raising a girl to womanhood; especially in this day and
age when so many of the morals and principles of God's word are no
longer honored by our society. Your Madison is at an age when she
will begin to determine her course in life. Talk to her about the
importance of purity and of finding a godly man for marriage.*

*If I have any regrets in my life, I'd say it was being busy with
ministry. I tried very hard to make Michelle's mother and
grandmother my top priority. But it was a continuous balancing act.
As I look back on it, I wonder if some of the heartaches Sheila
experienced in her marriage to John could have been avoided if I would
have somehow been even more present in her life.*

All that said, I see God's hand through it all. Sheila is my treasure. And my greatest joy was seeing her turn her life back over to God.

I hope you understand how important you are in the lives of your kids. It can be awkward at times with a girl. But a father has the ability to make his daughter feel like a princess. I know Madison feels that way. I hope she always will. And it's my hope that this little ring will be an important symbol for both of you until the day you find yourself at the altar giving your precious daughter's hand to the man of her dreams.

Joan and I didn't get a chance to raise a son. But if we would have, I'd like to think he would have been a lot like you. I'm so thankful you are Michelle's husband. She is a very blessed young woman. And Caleb will become a great man, if he follows your example. Keep up the good work, Steve.

With love,

Grandpa Phil

Joan nodded and handed the letter back to Steve. "Still preaching from the grave," she said with a smile.

Steve gave her a warm smile and showed the letter to Michelle. She read through it and then handed it back to him, giving him a hug as she did.

"Here's something for you, Grandma," Madison said as she handed a small package to Sheila.

Taped on the top of the box was a note from her father. She opened it, and read aloud, "These are some treasures my mother gave me to pass along to you. You may remember one of them from our little tea parties when you were a girl." She opened the box and pulled out a porcelain teacup and saucer. Inside the cup was a tiny velvet box. Carefully opening the hinged lid, she found a beautiful antique wedding band.

"Oh, my," Joan said. "That was your grandmother's wedding ring."

Sheila lifted the ring out of the box and slipped it onto her finger. It fit perfectly. Stretching out her hand and admiring it, she looked over at Joan. "Did you know about this, Mom?"

"I haven't seen that ring in years," she replied. "He must have been keeping it in his sock drawer with his father's pocket watch."

"Wait, there's something else," Sheila said as she lifted another envelope from the bottom of the box. Inside, she found a letter and a DVD. Scrawled across the front was a note. "These are things I want you to always remember, Princess."

She pulled out the letter and started reading it, but her tears prevented her from finishing. "I think I'll keep this until later," she said. "I wonder what's on the DVD."

"Let's watch it," Caleb said.

Sheila handed it to him, and he turned on the television, popping the DVD into the player. Immediately, Phil appeared on the screen.

"How on earth?" Joan said. Then she remembered her letter and how Phil had explained that the neighbor boy, Trent, had helped him with the gifts. "So this is how they make movies now?" she asked.

"Yep," Tim answered. "It's pretty easy actually."

As Phil began to speak, something stirred in Joan. "You know, honey," she said to Sheila, interrupting their focus, "I think maybe you'd best watch this yourself, first." She tipped her heads toward the children. "You can share it with us later."

Steve took the remote control from Caleb and pressed the pause button. He glanced at Sheila, who nodded in agreement. Ejecting the disc, he slipped it into the paper case and handed it to his mother-in-law.

"Well, your grandpa was certainly busy out there in the shed," Joan said to break the awkward silence.

"Is that all that's in there?" Caleb asked, seeming eager to play with all his new toys.

Steve peered into the box. "Looks like there's one more thing." He pulled out a large manila envelope with Joan's name on it. It appeared to be stuffed pretty full of some paperwork.

Her hands shook a little as she unfastened the tabs that hooked the flap down. The first thing she pulled out was another DVD pack. This one had two discs inside. She removed them and read the black marker on the face of each. "To share with family," one said. "For my sweetheart only," was written across the other.

"Well, let's have a look-see at this one," she said, handing the DVD to Tim. He popped it into the player and turned the television back on. Music filled the room as Phil and Joan's favorite melodies played in the background of a slideshow of photos from their entire marriage. Starting with images from their wedding and continuing with a myriad of scenes, their lives together were chronicled over a twenty-minute show.

One of Joan's favorite segments showed pictures from shortly after Sheila's birth. All in black and white, they captured some of her most treasured memories with her husband.

Finally, the music faded and the slides stopped. Then a recent picture of Phil appeared on the screen, holding a sign that said, "My love will never leave any of you. See you on the other side."

Joan smiled and sighed. "I think I'll save the rest of this for later," she said, gesturing to the pack of paperwork and the other DVD on her lap. "I'm so glad we got to all spend this Christmas together," she added, trying to sound cheerful as fatigue began to overtake her.

Sheila must have noticed her fading because she said, "I think we'll head back to our place now and get Josie settled in." She glanced over at Rick.

"I'll go load the cat into the carrier and put our things in the car," he said as he stood to his feet. Turning to

Michelle and Steve, he added, "Thank you for including me in this family Christmas. It means more to me than you can know."

Michelle smiled and nodded. "You are family, Rick. And in another week it will be official."

CHAPTER SIXTEEN

When Joan, Sheila, and Rick got back to Sheila's house, Rick set up the kitty's litter box in the bathroom. "Let's leave her in there for a little bit," Joan suggested, making a bed for Josie on the floor out of some old towels. "I need to lay down and rest, and it will give her a chance to get acclimated to her new place."

They closed the door carefully to avoid any possible paws that might be in the way. Josie was quiet, other than some scratching sounds in the litter box, so Joan said goodbye to Rick and gave her daughter a hug before going into her bedroom.

She placed the envelope from Phil on the dresser. The activities and emotions of the morning were more than she could handle without a short snooze. She wanted to be fresh when she pulled out the rest of the material her dear husband had left for her.

Stretching out on her bed, she closed her eyes and was asleep instantly. She slept soundly, dreamlessly for two hours. Then a soft knock on the door brought her back to consciousness.

Sheila stuck her head in the door, little Josie cradled in her arms. "Can we come in?"

Joan nodded and scooted herself up against the headboard.

"Someone was asking for you," her daughter said with a smile as she placed the puffy white kitten on her lap.

Joan smiled and stroked her soft fur eliciting a deep purr that seemed out of place in such a tiny body. "Have you been behaving yourself while I slept?" she asked Josie.

"She did great until about ten minutes ago," Sheila said. "We didn't hear a peep out of her. Then I heard a little scratching sound, and found her sticking her paw out under the bathroom door and feeling around on the carpet."

"You rascal," Joan said to the kitten. Then turning to Sheila, she asked, "How long did I sleep?"

"About two hours."

"Wow, I must have been really tired." She cuddled the kitty to her chest. "What time is the dinner tonight?"

"Michelle asked us to be there around six. Rick and I thought we'd take a little walk at the beach before then and peek into the chapel to see what the lighting is like this time of day."

"Oh. Is he still here? I thought he was going home for a while."

"I did, too. But we got to talking and making honeymoon plans, and so he decided to just stay here until we all go for dinner," Sheila explained. "Do you want me to make you some tea before we go for our walk?"

"That would be great, dear. And, do you think you or Rick could help me get the movie going on the television? I'd really like to watch whatever it is your father recorded for me."

"Sure, Mom," she replied with a smile. "I'll take Josie so you can freshen up, and we'll have some tea and get the TV ready for you in a few minutes." She reached down and lifted the kitty from Joan's lap, saying, "Come on, cutie pie. Let's go make some tea."

She opened the bedroom drapes to let the daylight stream in before leaving Joan alone to get up and get ready.

Joan swung her feet down to the floor and pushed off the mattress as she stood. "These old bones don't like to

130

move the way they used to," she muttered. Then she added, "But I guess I should be thankful for two legs and two arms that can still do their jobs."

Gazing in the mirror, she saw an old woman looking back at her. *It's funny, Lord, how part of me doesn't feel any different inside than I did when I was Michelle's age. But this mirror and these aches and pains don't lie. Soon I'll probably be seeing You, and my precious Phil, face-to-face.* She smiled at her own reflection, brushed her hair a little, and then picked up her envelope and headed out to the front room.

Rick was down on one knee in front of the television, inserting the DVD into the player on the lower shelf of the cabinet. He stood as she entered the room and asked if she'd had a good rest.

"Yes. I feel much better, although still a little groggy," she replied.

"This should help," Sheila said, entering from the kitchen with a teacup in her hand. She set it down on the little table beside the rocking chair where Joan always loved to sit.

"Thanks, dear. Where's Josie?" Joan asked.

Just then, the little kitten came bounding out of the hallway from the direction of the bathroom.

"I put her in the litter box one more time to make sure she knew where it was. I think she'll be fine if we leave the bathroom door open when no one's in there," Sheila replied.

The white furball darted around the room, leapt on the couch, and then jumped off again.

"Be careful where you walk, Mom. She's so tiny right now. I don't want you to trip."

"I'll watch for her, honey. Don't worry. We'll be fine."

Rick used the remote control to turn on the television and showed Joan how to begin playing the DVD. "The volume control works just like when you are watching a regular show," he reminded her, indicating the up and down arrows. "And when you are ready to stop the movie or to pause it, you can just push this button."

"Do you think you'll want to watch regular TV after you see Dad's DVD?" Sheila asked.

"No. I think I'll read through this material when it's over," Joan replied, lifting the envelope.

"Okay, then all you need to do after you stop the DVD is to hit the power button and the television will shut off," Rick said.

Sheila picked up her purse and jacket and said, "We'll be back in about an hour or so."

"Have fun," Joan said, lifting her teacup to take a sip as she settled into the rocker for her movie.

Rick hit the play button on the remote. "Here goes," he said, as he handed the device to Joan. "See you soon, Mom."

Mom. That sounded nice coming from her future son-in-law.

Just as the front door closed behind them, an image of Phil, sitting in the shed on a stool, appeared before Joan, filling the television screen. He looked away from the camera for a moment and asked, "So it's recording now?"

She could hear Trent's voice in the background. "Yep. You're on."

"Okay, thanks." She saw Trent dip his head down and wave goodbye into the camera, and then she heard the shed door close.

Phil's eyes seemed to be gazing straight into hers. She sat forward in the rocker, leaning close to him.

"Hello, Jo. You've probably already had a chance to look at the other contents of the envelope I'm leaving you for Christmas."

Oh no. Should I have looked at those first?

Her husband continued. "You may think you want to read all of them at once. But I hope you'll follow our old rules and do what it says on each envelope."

That old coot must have written some cards for various occasions!
She smiled at the thought.

"As you can see, Trent's been helping me out here in the shed. It was his idea to make the movies. Good thing the youngsters these days are born with natural skills in technology. I never would have been able to figure out this newfangled system."

She smiled as she watched his eyes crinkle in a humble grin.

"I've been thinking about all the things I want to say to you here. But how do I put into words a lifetime of gratefulness?" He paused and took a deep breath. "We made it, Jo. We made it all the way to the end. Remember what Bob Hope used to say, 'You know you're getting old when the candles cost more than the cake.'"

She chuckled softly. "Yes, I remember that one, Phil."

He sat back on his stool a little, grasping a raised knee for balance. "Remember that camping trip to the lake for our first anniversary?"

"Yes. It rained the whole time," she said.

"It rained the whole week," he echoed. "But you were such a good sport as we snuggled in our tent and cooked dinner under umbrellas."

She nodded, smiling at the memory.

"I knew I had captured myself a great gal after that week." He paused and looked into the camera as if sitting right there looking into her eyes.

Joan's heart leapt into her throat. Suddenly they were twenty-one again and so very much in love. So many memories came flooding back. The twinkle in his eye, his gentle touch, and the way he could always make her smile.

"Aside from the day I made you my bride, I'd have to say the very best day of my life was when we became parents," Phil continued. "I remember watching them whisk you away to the delivery room. I thought I'd wear a hole in that gray linoleum floor with my pacing." He looked down at his hands and then back through the camera to her heart. "Seeing you, with our tiny baby girl in your arms...well...I'll just never forget that moment."

She nodded. And suddenly she could actually feel Sheila, as a helpless newborn, snuggled to her chest. Tears of joy mingled with tears of longing for just one more moment with them all together as a family.

Phil's voice caught her attention again. "I'd have to say that the hardest day of my life was when we had to say goodbye to Christopher." His voice caught and she saw him swallow a lump of sorrow. "I suppose I'll be seeing him again soon, though, sweetheart. And I'll be sure to tell him all about you."

Visions of their stillborn son flashed through Joan's mind. Images she'd buried deep inside and rarely shared with anyone. She tried to imagine Phil meeting their little boy on the other side. What must that reunion have been like? And what would it be like for her to see them both together one day?

Phil's posture on the screen straightened as he took a deep breath and continued. "I'm sure you'll remember that scrappy little puppy I brought home the week after Christopher's funeral. Sheila sure did love that little guy. They were inseparable."

Memories of Sheila toddling around, trying to carry Riley Rover through the house brought a smile back to Joan's face. That puppy was such a gift from God at a time when they really needed a boost of joy in their hearts.

A twinkle returned to Phil's eye. "Hey, remember when I helped Sheila pull out her front tooth, and you had to leave the room?"

She laughed and wagged her finger at the screen. "You really had me going with that string tied to her tooth," she scolded the man on the screen.

Phil cleared his throat and looked right into her soul. "You've always had such a tender heart, Jo. It's another thing I've treasured in you even though it meant I was in charge of cleaning and bandaging those scraped knees and elbows."

Joan nodded. *I'm so glad you were willing to do that, Phil. But you'll never know how many times I had to do it myself, too.*

He went on to reminisce about how they served side-by-side in premarital counseling for the church, and how valuable her input was as they guided young engaged folks into a lifelong commitment.

Phil dropped his foot to the floor and sat forward again. "I know I wasn't always the perfect husband, Jo. I got so wrapped up in ministry from time to time, and left you home alone more nights than I should have."

Joan wracked her memory. All she could think of was his faithfulness to be there with her and Sheila at nearly every dinner.

As if reading her thoughts, he said, "I guess I was pretty good about getting home for your cooking," he chuckled, "but there were too many nights I had to leave again to go to a hospital or attend a church meeting. I know those things were important, and I believe God called me to do them. But this heart," he said, tapping his chest, "this old ticker sure wishes I could get those nights back and spend them with you now." His voice cracked as he finished speaking.

Tears filled Joan's eyes. "It's alright, dear. I understand."

Phil leaned back and stretched his leg forward so he could pull a hanky out of his front pant pocket. Blowing his nose, he composed himself and continued. "So, it looks like we'll be apart for a spell here." He winced, and she remembered the pain he experienced those last few months.

"God's calling me home, Jo." Again his eyes looked directly at her. "I want you to spend however much time you have left, *really living*, Joan. I mean it. Don't waste a moment. Seek God and ask Him what His purpose is for your remaining time on earth. Don't let age rob you of whatever He might have planned."

It was something she hadn't expected to hear from him. Memories, yes. But this? His words reminded her of the impression she'd gotten back home in Mariposa. A purpose. *Do you really have a purpose for me to fulfill even now?* she asked God silently.

And a whisper in her spirit said, *Yes.*

"I love you, Jo. You have been all I could have ever wanted in a wife and even more. There was not a single day that I did not thank God for bringing you into my life."

"I love you, too, Phil," she whispered.

He leaned really close to the camera and added, "I'll see you on the other side. You won't need to look for me because I'll be at the front of the crowd to welcome you home."

Joan watched through the tears, as her husband blew her a kiss and then disappeared, replaced by a blank screen on the television.

She sat still for a long time, soaking in his smile and words. Then she lifted the envelope from the table and slid the contents out. A stack of cards and letters rested on her lap, each marked with a significant event. Anniversaries, birthdays, even Valentine's Day—he remembered them all and had envelopes marked for her to open on each important day for the next few years.

Reaching for the remote control, she pressed the play button again. As she hoped, the DVD began at the beginning. She watched it several times, each time feeling a little more nostalgic and yet lighter in her spirit. It was a gift she would treasure for the rest of her earthly life.

CHAPTER SEVENTEEN

The week between Christmas and New Years flew by in a blur of preparations. When they weren't focused on the wedding and reception, they were discussing and planning Joan's move to Shoreline Manor. Rick even created floor plans with graph paper, and Sheila and Joan played with furniture arrangements for the living area and bedroom.

Josie was settling in to her new home and family. Joan purchased a few toys, and they all enjoyed a lot of laughs watching the busy little kitten throwing her toy mice in the air and pouncing on a feather teaser as Joan jiggled it on the floor.

"You're going to have a lot of fun with her, Mom," Sheila said, looking very satisfied with Rick's gift.

"She does make me smile," Joan admitted.

Sheila had arranged for Madison to come and stay with Joan while she and Rick were out of town. "She'll be good company for you and Josie."

A couple of days before the wedding, Joan and her daughter planned meals and went to the market. "Michelle will pick up anything else you need, Mom. Don't hesitate to call her. She has to buy groceries herself once or twice a week anyway."

Sheila and Rick stood at the doorway, saying goodnight. "I can't wait for tomorrow," he murmured softly into her ear. "You'll be the most beautiful bride in the world."

She smiled. "One of the oldest."

"Not in my eyes. You make me feel like a kid again," he said, taking both her hands in his. "I hope I can do this right," he added.

"Do what?" she asked, her heart stopping for a moment.

"Be the kind of husband you deserve," he replied. "It's going to be quite a learning curve for this old bachelor."

Relief washed over her, and she laughed softly. "Well, so far, Dr. Chambers, I'd say you're off to a good start."

"Why thank you," he replied with a grin. "And tomorrow, it'll be Dr. and Mrs. Chambers."

Sheila just looked at him for a moment, once again taking in the amazing truth that she was marrying this man. "I can hardly wait. It will be my honor to wear your name."

As he kissed her goodnight, an image from her childhood flashed through her mind of her parents kissing goodbye before her father went to the church office each morning. And she realized she hadn't had a chance to watch the DVD he'd left behind for her. *Tonight's the night,* she thought as she gave Rick a final hug.

"See you at the chapel," she said.

"I'll be waiting," he replied.

Teeth brushed, face washed, and nightgown and robe donned, Sheila settled down on the couch and flipped on the television, careful to keep the volume low so she wouldn't awaken her mother, who was sleeping soundly in the guest room.

She inserted her father's DVD into the player and pushed the start button on the remote control.

As soon as she saw his face, her eyes filled with tears. And his voice, so familiar and comforting, filled not only her ears but also her very heart and mind.

"My darling daughter. How can I put into words all the thoughts and feelings I want to share with you?

"You and your mother are the light of my life. The greatest gifts God ever gave this old fellow. I hope you know that.

"There's never been a day I didn't find myself thanking Him for the honor and privilege of being your dad. Each heartache and joy you've experienced, well you need to know I've experienced them right along with you.

"You've had more than your share of hurts, honey. I blame some of that on myself. If only I'd somehow helped you see how difficult life would be married to a non-believer, like John. God knows I tried. But I often wonder, did I try hard enough? To reach out to him as well as advise you?"

Sheila hit the pause button. "Oh, Dad," she said to the face on the screen. "There's no way you could have dissuaded me from marrying him." She thought back over the many years of struggles in her marriage, especially the desperate act of trying to take his own life that John had committed in the not so distant past.

Then she thought about her dad's steady love and compassion, and how he'd intervened and actually led her husband to the foot of the cross. "You did well, Dad. And I love you for it."

After taking a deep breath, she pushed play again. "My great consolation is the wonderful grandchildren you and John gave us." His voice cracked as he added, "I never realized how deeply I'd love them. Being a grandfather took me by surprise."

She smiled, remembering the first time she'd placed Michelle in her father's arms. He held her tentatively at first, which surprised her because she'd seen him cradle many a newborn at church dedications. But this one was hers. And she could see the difference in his countenance and posture.

"It's okay, Dad. She won't break," she'd said.

And he'd leaned down and breathed in the fragrance of her newborn daughter. When he looked back up, his eyes were brimming with tears.

Drawn back to her father's voice, she focused again on the screen in front of her and joined her father in a sweet time of reminiscing about their family. Vacations, special events, and priceless moments the two of them had shared. It was almost like having him sitting there with her, remembering it all together.

And then the focus switched to the present.

"I know you and Rick are getting very serious, sweetheart. And I want you to know that I have a good feeling about him. Sometimes the people who become the closest to God are the ones who've pushed Him away for most of their lives. When the walls are broken down, and they see Him face-to-face in His Word, and sense His spirit tugging on their hearts, they discover a love they will cling to fiercely from that point on.

"I believe your professor friend is one of those converts. He knows life without God, and now he knows life with Him. There's no turning back. He will stay the course to the end. I really believe that. And it blesses me to think that you may end up making that journey with him.

"If it comes to that, and the two of you marry, I want you to know that you have my blessing. It saddens me to think of missing that event, of not being able to be your dad and walk you down the aisle once again. But know that my love will be there. And as surely as I will be holding onto Jesus on the other side, as long as you and Rick do the same, we will be linked in spirit."

Sheila nodded, tears streaming down her face. And although he wouldn't be present in the flesh tomorrow, she knew a part of him would be there in her heart.

"I love you more than words can say, Sheila. And I will be forever grateful you were my daughter.

"Take care of your mother. And I'll see you on the other side, princess."

Then the screen went blank.

⁑

After a long, nearly sleepless night, Sheila awakened to the sound of her mother stirring around. She arose from bed and joined her in the kitchen for coffee and breakfast.

The morning flew by. Then it was time to get ready.

Sheila had bought Joan a new dress and helped her into it, pinning a corsage on as well. "You look beautiful, Mom."

"You do too, sweetheart," she replied as she examined her daughter's simple, but elegant, plum colored lace dress. "I wish your father could see you now."

Sheila nodded, pulling her into a hug as she thought about the DVD. She wanted to tell her mother about watching it last night. But something held her back. Instead she just replied, "I wish he were here, too."

The ceremony took place at four o'clock at the little chapel by the lighthouse. With the sound of waves crashing on the shore and heavy storm clouds blanketing the coast line, Sheila and Rick stood holding hands as Ben led them in a simple exchange of wedding vows. Michelle and Madison stood off to the side of Sheila, and Rick had requested that Steve and Caleb stand up for him.

Tim, who was still in Sandy Cove, escorted Joan to her seat and then walked his mother up the aisle, giving her hand to his soon-to-be stepfather, Rick. Then he took his seat, with Joan on one side, and Kelly and her brood on the other. Tim's girlfriend Traci, a photographer by hobby, snapped pictures as the bride and groom slipped rings onto each other's fingers and exchanged their first kiss as husband and wife.

After about a dozen family photos, the group headed for their dinner celebration at the Cliffhanger Restaurant, dodging raindrops that had begun to fall.

As they took their seats in the banquet room overlooking the stormy surf, Joan's heart swelled with joy for her daughter, who looked youthful and radiant. She couldn't help but notice Rick's attentiveness, pulling out Sheila's chair, focusing on her throughout the conversation, and occasionally leaning over and whispering in her ear.

The meal was delicious, and a small but beautifully decorated wedding cake was the dessert.

Steve presented a toast, and Tim chimed in with a few comments of his own. As the waiter began to serve the cake, Caleb tugged on Michelle's arm. "Mommy?" he began.

"Yes?"

Then, in a voice loud enough for all to hear, he asked, "Is Dr. Chambers my grandpa now?"

A look of surprise swept around the table. Michelle glanced over at her former professor, who seemed eager to hear her reply. Nodding to her son, she said, "Yes, honey. He is."

Immediately a look of gratitude and love washed over Sheila's face, and Rick beamed as he made eye contact with Michelle and winked.

"Okay, good," Caleb replied, unfazed by the emotions of the adults surrounding him. "So can we fly my new plane at the beach when you and Grandma get back from your vacation, Grandpa?" he asked.

Rick glanced at Michelle, who nodded. Then turning to Caleb, he replied, "We sure can, son."

CHAPTER EIGHTEEN

Joan spent a delightful week with Madison while Sheila and Rick were in California for their honeymoon. At first she'd balked at the idea of needing someone to stay with her. But, as it turned out, she was thankful Sheila had insisted.

Maddie loved to cook, and the two of them baked cookies, pies, and banana bread. They watched family videos and old classics on television, played with Josie and laughed at her antics, and took leisurely walks at the beach on days when the weather allowed.

Something about Maddie reminded Joan of Sheila as a young girl. Maybe it was her light coloring with that strawberry blonde hair and blue eyes. While most people remarked how much she looked like her father with his sandy hair and matching eyes, Joan saw Sheila in her great granddaughter's smile. And this week that they shared together, reminded Joan of being a young mother with her daughter by her side.

She relished every moment.

Soon Sheila and Rick would be back, and Madison's Christmas break would be over. Then Joan would be moving to Shoreline Manor. Although she knew it was for the best, she couldn't help but feel a little nervous about starting over in a new home, with new neighbors, and living apart from family.

Of course, Sheila and Michelle both insisted she'd be spending much of her time with them anyway. And since Joan didn't drive, she knew she'd be relying on her daughter and granddaughter to help her get to the market, medical appointments, and wherever else she needed to go. But at the end of every day, when it was time to go to bed, she'd be alone.

"Oh, Phil. I do miss you something awful," she found herself confessing one night after Madison had gone to sleep. She picked up a framed photo of her husband that Sheila kept on the buffet. Gazing into his eyes, Joan had the sensation he was watching her from somewhere above.

She remembered before he died, how he'd referred to the scripture from Hebrews of a great cloud of witnesses cheering believers to their final finish line in life. "I'll be right there in the front row," he'd promised.

Looking his photo squarely in the eye, she said, "I'm counting on you, honey." Then she placed the picture back in its place and turned in for the night. As she lowered herself to her knees beside the bed, Joan asked God to give her husband a hug for her. *And Christopher, too, Lord,* she prayed silently in the secret places of her heart. She thanked Him for the sweet week with her great granddaughter and asked for strength for what was ahead. *Please fulfill Your plan for the days ahead,* she added, thinking not only of her move, but also of each of the members of her family who were so dear to her.

Then grasping the nightstand with one hand and the bed with the other, she eased herself off the floor, pulled back the quilt, and slipped between the sheets. Hugging her blanket and Phil's pillow tightly to her body, she drifted off to sleep.

Sunday came too quickly, and after a pancake breakfast together, Joan and Madison got ready for church. Maddie would be returning home that night since school started again the next day. Sheila and Rick were due home late that afternoon, so Michelle offered to feed everyone dinner.

"Are you sure you're up for that, what with going back to school yourself tomorrow?" Joan asked when Michelle came to pick them up to take them to church.

"I already put ingredients for stew into the crockpot, Grandma. There's nothing else I need to do except make some biscuits."

"Let us do that, Mom," Madison piped up from the back of the van.

Joan agreed. "Madison and I have had fun baking all week. We've gotten to be good partners in the kitchen."

"You've got a deal," Michelle said.

So after church, Joan changed her clothes and left a note on the counter for Sheila saying she'd be at Steve and Michelle's house baking biscuits with Madison.

Soon the two of them were measuring and mixing the dough, flouring the cutting board and rolling pin, rolling it out, and cutting the biscuits with an upside down juice glass.

"Wow," Michelle said, as she came into the room to stir the stew. "You two are really making some nice biscuits there. I usually just scoop out spoonfuls and drop them onto the cookie sheet, but yours look very professional."

Madison smiled proudly. "Grandma Joan knows how to cook the old-fashioned way. That's how I want to cook when I'm the mom."

Joan beamed at the compliment. What a joy to watch another generation take up the baton and learn the skills her mother and grandmother had patiently taught her.

"I think that's wonderful, Madison," her mother replied. "Maybe you can help me refine my skills, too," she added with a wink.

"Sure smells good in here," Steve said as he strolled into the kitchen. "Those biscuits look great," he added, draping his arm over his daughter's shoulder. "You're learning from the best, you know," he said, tipping his head toward Joan.

"I know, Dad. Great Grandma and I have been cooking all week."

"Nice. Did you bring any goodies home for your old man?"

"Show him," Joan said.

Madison walked over to the counter and opened two plastic storage containers. One had two dozen chocolate chip cookies. "Made from scratch," she said as she showed her father. The other had an apple pie with a flawless lattice top crust.

"There goes my waistline," Steve replied, patting his stomach with both hands.

Michelle laughed and hugged him from behind. "Madison's learning to cook just like her great grandmother. So you'd better start working out or practicing some portion control," she added with a wink.

Caleb bounded into the room followed by Thumper, close at his heels. "I think Grandma and Grandpa are here," he said. "Some car just pulled into the driveway." Grabbing one of the chocolate chip cookies before anyone could say a word, he bolted upstairs, hollering, "I'm going to get my airplane."

Steve looked a little puzzled. "What's that about?"

"Remember what Rick said at the dinner reception? About how they could fly it together when he got back?" Michelle replied.

"That boy doesn't miss a beat," Joan said with a chuckle.

"Poor Dr. Chambers," Madison said, rolling her eyes.

"I'm not feeling so poor," Rick said as he and Sheila walked into the kitchen hand in hand.

"Welcome home, Mom." Michelle held out her arms and the two women embraced. "Did you have a good time in California?"

Sheila smiled and nodded. "Wonderful. It was warm and sunny. We had a beautiful suite overlooking the ocean." Then she turned to Joan. "Hi, Mom. How are you doing?"

"Good. Real good. Madison and I had a fun week together doing lots of baking. We're just finishing up with these biscuits. Help yourself to a cookie if you'd like." She nudged Madison, who extended the treats to both Sheila and Rick.

"I found it! I found it!" Caleb cried happily as he ran back into the kitchen, his new red airplane in hand.

"Well, look at that," Sheila said to Rick. "Guess your number is up."

"I've been waiting all week for this, Caleb," Rick said as he ruffled the boy's hair. "Let's leave these ladies in the kitchen and do some serious flying."

Caleb beamed. Turning to Steve, he added, "You, too, Dad," as he grabbed his father's hand.

CHAPTER NINETEEN

"Have you seen Josie, Sheila?" Joan asked that night after they'd gotten home from Michelle's house. "She followed me into the bedroom," Rick said, returning from taking his and Sheila's luggage in there. "I think she's under the bed."

"I'll get her, Mom," Sheila offered. Joan noticed her daughter's hand brush against Rick's as she headed for their room. A moment later, Sheila returned with the little ball of fur in her arms. "Where would you like her?"

"She's in a routine of sleeping in my bathroom now," Joan replied. "You'll see her little bed in there near the tub." Joan reached out and stroked her new pet. "Time to go to bed, little one." The kitten purred contentedly. "I guess I'll turn in early, too," Joan added. "I'm sure you have a lot of unpacking to do and getting settled in." She smiled warmly at her daughter and new son-in-law.

"Okay, Mom. See you in the morning," Sheila replied.

"Goodnight," Rick added, standing awkwardly by his bride. After Joan went into her bedroom and closed the door, she could hear him add, "It seems strange to be living here now. I'm so used to saying goodnight to you at the door," he tipped his head in the direction of the front door, "and heading back to my place."

"Is that what you'd like to do?" Sheila asked teasingly.

"Not after last week," he replied. Joan could imagine his expression as he gazed at her daughter.

And then it was quiet.

These walls are pretty thin. I never noticed that before, she thought. Then she remembered she'd forgotten to bring a glass of water to bed with her. She liked to keep one on the nightstand in case she awoke thirsty during the night. *Should I go back out there?* She sat on the foot of the bed, uncertain what to do. Some murmuring of voices drifted through the wall, but she couldn't make out what they were saying. Then she heard Sheila's bedroom door close. *Okay, guess this is my chance.* She cracked open her door and could see that the living room lights were turned out.

As she walked quietly past Sheila's room, she could hear Rick talking about unpacking their bags. "Let's wait until morning," her daughter replied.

Not wanting to eavesdrop, Joan scooted quickly out to the front room, nearly tripping over the ottoman beside the couch. She made her way cautiously through the dark and into the kitchen when a voice startled her.

"Are you okay, Mom?"

Joan's hand flew to her chest as she whipped around to face her daughter. "You scared me," she replied.

"Sorry about that. I just came out to get my cosmetic bag. I left it in here when we unloaded the car." She put her hand on Joan's shoulder. "Can I get you something? Some tea maybe?"

"No, dear. I'm fine. I just came out to get a glass of water." Joan kissed her daughter's cheek. "Goodnight."

The next morning, Joan arose to the high-pitched crying of her little kitty. "I'm coming, Josie," she called softly as she slipped on her robe. Exiting the bedroom, she nearly bumped into Rick, who was looking down at his tie as he cinched the knot upward.

"Excuse me," he blurted, his face blushing slightly. "I wasn't looking where I was going."

Joan smiled. "It's fine. Looks like you're in a hurry."

"Unfortunately, I've got an early meeting at the college, and we overslept a little."

"Is Sheila up?" Joan asked.

"She's making coffee, I think."

The sound of Josie's cries intensified. "I'd better attend to her," Joan remarked, glancing at the bathroom door. "I hope you have a good day at work, Rick."

"Thanks," he replied, giving her a smile and heading for the kitchen.

When Joan got inside the bathroom, she scooped Josie up and nuzzled her close. "We'll be moving soon, kitty," she said, as much to herself as to the little ball of fur.

As she carried her into the kitchen, she caught Sheila and Rick saying goodbye, interrupting what looked like a lingering kiss. "I'm so sorry," she said. "I thought you'd left."

"On my way," he replied, winking at Sheila and then giving Joan a warm smile. "See you two tonight."

Sheila followed him to the door leading into the garage and watched his car pull out, waving one more time. Then she turned to Joan. "What would you like for breakfast?"

They settled on English muffins and then sat together at the breakfast nook to discuss their day. "I think we should go over to Shoreline Manor and make sure everything is set for my move next week," Joan suggested. She imagined her daughter was eager was to get into a routine with her new husband.

"Okay, Mom. That sounds like a good idea. Your furniture and boxes are scheduled for delivery a week from Saturday, so Steve and Rick will both be able to help."

After eating and getting dressed, they took off for Joan's future home. *Please God, help me adjust to this new life,* she prayed silently as her daughter drove through town.

The receptionist at the Shoreline Manor office was cheerful, casting a ray of sunshine on the otherwise gloomy winter day. "Joan Walker, right?" she asked with a smile as she retrieved a file of folders from the corner of her desk. "Yes. That's right," Joan replied. "I'm to move in a week from this weekend."

Flipping through the paperwork in her file, the girl replied, "It looks like all the cleaning and repairs have been made. Would you like to go take a look?"

Joan felt a mixture of uneasiness and curiosity. Glancing at Sheila, who nodded in response, she replied, "Yes. I think we'd like to do that."

"If you'll just wait here for a moment, I'll get someone to take you," she replied. She disappeared behind a closed door, and a minute later a gentleman appeared and greeted them.

"My name is Travis. I'll be happy to take you over to your unit, Mrs. Walker." A large key ring dangled from his left hand as he stretched out his right one to shake theirs. "This way, please," he continued, leading them out through a pair of glass double doors and along the paved walkway that wound through the complex. "Looks like we might get some rain this afternoon," he commented.

"I think you're right," Sheila agreed.

Joan pulled her sweater closed as the cold breeze caused a sudden chill.

Soon they were at the front door of her apartment. Travis slipped the key into the lock and swung the door open. Although the temperature inside was not warm, it was better than the drafty walkway. Joan hurried in, followed closely by her daughter.

The scents of new carpet smell, mingled with bleach and lemon oil, greeted Joan as her eyes swept the front room. It looked even smaller than she remembered. Turning to Sheila, she asked, "Do you think I'll be able to fit my sofa and coffee table in here?"

Her daughter smiled reassuringly. "We measured it out, remember? Everything you wanted the movers to bring will fit just fine."

Joan nodded skeptically.

"Let's walk through all the rooms," her daughter suggested.

"Be my guest," Travis replied, gesturing to the rest of the apartment. "I'll just wait here. Take as long as you need, and if you find anything that concerns you, please let me know. We'll be happy to take care of it."

As Joan glanced into the kitchen, she smiled. "I really like how this room looks over the dining area and living room. Our old kitchen felt a little isolated."

"I think you'll really enjoy that, Mom. It's pretty popular these days."

"And you're sure we measured for my dining room table?"

"I'm sure. It will fit fine here as long as you don't have the leaves in it."

Joan nodded. "Okay. I won't be needing those anyway."

When they walked into the bedroom, Sheila noticed the closet door wasn't hanging right. "I'll be right back, Mom." She left to go get Travis, and Joan stood in the doorway trying to imagine her bedroom furniture in this room.

When Sheila pointed out the closet door to their escort, he pulled his radio off his belt loop and called the maintenance crew. "I need someone over in unit 17 to take a look at a door." Then he turned to both ladies. "They'll get that fixed today. I'll make sure of it."

The bathroom looked smaller than Sheila's guest bath. "Do you think I'll have room for Josie's litter box and bed in here?" Joan asked.

"Hmmm. Maybe not."

Travis cleared his throat. "Not to interfere, but several of our tenants have cats, and I've noticed they often set up those items in the utility room by the back door."

"Utility room?" Joan asked.

"The laundry room, Mom. Let's go take a look."

Travis pointed to one corner of the small space. "If you put a stacking washer dryer unit here, you have some floor space left next to it."

Joan looked at Sheila. "I was planning to use my old washer and dryer."

"I know. But he's got a point. Maybe we should sell those and get you a stacking set. Then Josie could have her room in here, too. Besides, I like that idea for nighttime. Then she isn't underfoot when you wake up and need to use the bathroom."

Joan nodded. "Okay. Let's see what those stacking units run."

Sheila smiled at her. "We can go after we leave here."

As they walked back through the apartment on their way to the front door, Joan prayed silently for God's plan as she prepared to begin this new chapter of her life.

"I think you'll enjoy living here," Sheila said reassuringly. " It'll be a fresh start for you, and it will be great to have you finally settled here in Sandy Cove."

CHAPTER TWENTY

After their visit to Shoreline Manor, Sheila and Joan purchased a stacking washer and dryer for her new apartment and they were able to notify the movers in time to have the old units left behind at the house. Sheila and Rick would be managing the listing and rental of Joan's home, and they suggested offering the washer and dryer to any potential tenants.

Joan tried to keep herself busy during the rest of her stay at Sheila's house. She got out her knitting and spent more time in the guest room knitting, watching television, and reading her Bible. Although she did join Sheila and Rick for meals, she tried to keep herself out of their way the rest of the time.

"You're not bothering us, Mom. We love having you around," Sheila said, and Rick agreed. But Joan wanted to get used to being alone. Besides, she had Josie to keep her company in the bedroom.

Finally the day of her move arrived. Rick left right after breakfast to pick up Steve and head over to meet the moving van. Sheila helped Joan pack her remaining clothes and toiletries into suitcases. "We'll just leave Josie's things here for now, Mom," Sheila said. "She's better off not being underfoot today. We can bring her and her gear over later."

"Good idea, honey," Joan replied.

When they arrived at the apartment, the furniture was being placed in each room. Sheila quickly took charge, instructing the men about the placement of each item and consulting with Joan whenever there was a question. Next the kitchen boxes were brought in and stacked on counters and the dining room table. Then boxes of linens and other miscellaneous items like lamps and books were unloaded. Joan was amazed at her daughter's efficiency as she instructed Steve and Rick in the unloading process. Soon the apartment began to take on the look of a home, with a cozy seating arrangement in the living room, a sleep-ready bedroom, and a well-stocked bathroom.

Michelle and Madison arrived around noon, bringing deli sandwiches for all as well as a flat of water bottles and some cookies. With Caleb occupied at his friend's house and all the heavy lifting and moving completed, the men settled down with their lunches and flipped on Joan's television to watch a basketball game, while the ladies ate and strategized the unpacking of the boxes and stocking the kitchen.

It took Michelle and Madison a couple of hours to line all the kitchen shelves and drawers. Sheila and Joan used that time to work in the bedroom and bathroom, emptying boxes and suitcases while they chatted about how well everything seemed to fit.

By the middle of the afternoon, the four females were unloading all the kitchen gear. Plates, glasses, pots, pans, utensils, cutlery, and silverware all found new homes.

"There's more storage here than I thought," Joan said with a smile.

"Need any help in here?" Steve asked, as he came to grab the cookie tin.

"Perfect timing, honey," Michelle replied. "We just finished."

"Let's send them to the market," Sheila said. She retrieved a small notepad from her purse and made a list of the essentials Joan would need for the night and morning. "Are you sure you don't want to come back to my place just for tonight?" she asked her mother.

"No. I want to stay here. But I do want to get Josie first."

"Right. We'll have the men stop at the house and pick her up on their way back here," Sheila replied, taking her list to Rick. "Honey, would you and Steve please go and pick up these items at the grocery store and then pick up the kitten and her gear on your way back?"

Rick looked at Steve, who nodded. "Okay." He took the list, and they left.

"Our turn to sit down," Michelle said. "Why don't I make us some tea and we can enjoy a few of those cookies ourselves."

As they sat around Joan's dining room table, Sheila asked how things were going at school.

"I've got a great group of kids this year," Michelle replied. "But I guess Caleb's teacher is having some struggles. She's got mostly boys. Nineteen out of the twenty-eight in the class. She sent out an email to all the parents yesterday asking for volunteers to come help out, especially during the reading instruction. I wish I could help her."

"Maybe I could do it," Sheila offered. "I'm no teacher, but I'd be happy to do whatever I can."

"She's mostly looking for other adults to sit one-on-one with kids who are struggling and listen to them read aloud, helping them out when they get stuck."

"Sounds easy," her mother said.

Joan listened, wondering if she should offer, too. Phil's words about finding her purpose came back to her. "Do you think she'd take an old lady like me?" she asked Michelle.

"I think she'd be thrilled to have you, Grandma," Michelle replied, "and Caleb would be so excited to have you two helping in his class."

"Why don't you send his teacher an email and find out if she'd like us to come together," Sheila suggested, sounding excited about the idea of volunteering with Joan.

"I'll do that and let you know," she promised.

"Did you tell Michelle about the boxes of Dad's sermons?" Sheila asked.

"Is that what all those file boxes are in your garage, Mom?" Michelle asked.

"Yep. Your grandmother was wondering if Ben might be interested in having them."

Suddenly it seemed like a silly idea to Joan. Almost as if she thought their pastor was a novice. "I've also thought about going through them and compiling some kind of devotional book for all of you," she said.

"I love that idea, Grandma. Maybe we could work on it together during the summer," Michelle replied enthusiastically.

"Really?" Joan asked.

"Sure! I would love to do that."

And again, a surge of joy found its way into Joan's heart.

That evening, after they'd all shared a pizza and salad dinner, Joan found herself alone in her new home, with Josie curled up on her lap. She was just about to watch a little television, when her doorbell rang.

"I wonder who that could be?" she said to her little friend.

As she opened the door, she was greeted by another woman, who looked to be about her age. "Hi there. My name's Margie," she said with a warm smile. "I live next door, and I just wanted to welcome you to Shoreline and give you these." She held out a basket, pulling back a cloth napkin to reveal some blueberry muffins. "I made them myself. From scratch," she added proudly.

Joan welcomed her into her apartment, introduced herself, and offered Margie a cup of tea.

"That sounds delightful," the woman replied with a slight brogue. "And let's have a muffin while they are warm."

Soon they were chatting about Shoreline Manor and finding out about each other's lives. "So I take it you are a widow, too," Margie said.

Joan nodded. "My Phil went home to be with the Lord not too long ago."

"It's been five years for me. Bobby was a minister for nearly fifty years. We always planned to travel after we retired, but…well…how do you get a man to retire from something that's so deeply engrained in his heart?"

"I know exactly what you mean. Phil was a pastor, too. He did retire from full-time work at the church, but he had a little congregation he ministered to at the local Alzheimer's home."

As they sat together swapping tales about their lives as pastors' wives, Joan was pleased with how much they had in common.

"I think you'll like it here," Margie said. "There are many good churches in the area, and Shoreline provides van transportation to all of them."

Joan told her about Ben's church and her family who lived in the area.

"How wonderful for you to be so close to your daughter and granddaughter! I do miss my son and his family. But they had to move to the east coast for business. So I count on my church ladies and friends here at Shoreline to be my second family," Margie said. Then she glanced at the kitchen clock. "Just look at the time, will you? And here I am chatting on while you are probably exhausted from your move."

"Actually, you've been welcome company, hasn't she, Josie?" Joan replied, scooping up the kitten from the floor. "What an adorable little kitty." Margie reached over and stroked the kitten's soft fur. "Well, I'd better be going. But let's have lunch together one day soon. I make a pretty mean chicken salad sandwich," she added with a wink. "And you keep these." She gestured toward the muffins. "You can return the basket later."

After she'd left, Joan went into her bedroom to get ready for bed. Although she'd dreaded this first night on her own, she didn't feel alone anymore. "I made a new friend today, Phil," she said to his picture on her nightstand before she knelt down to pray.

CHAPTER TWENTY-ONE

Joan's pulse quickened as she and Sheila walked into Caleb's classroom for their first day as volunteers. The teacher, Mrs. Harding, was just giving the children instructions about their independent seatwork to be done while the reading groups met in the back.

"I see that our volunteers have arrived," she said as all eyes in the room locked on Joan and her daughter. "Caleb, would you please come to the front and introduce your grandmother and great grandmother to all of us?"

Caleb glanced around at his classmates and smiled. He seemed at ease with the attention and was quick to take center stage up by the whiteboard. Taking Sheila by the hand, he led her to the middle of the room. "This is my Grandma Sheila." Then he tugged on her arm and whispered something to her. Listening to her response and nodding, he added, "You can call her 'Mrs. Chambers'."

Joan was so used to her daughter being Sheila Ackerman that it took a moment for her to process her new married name. Upon the teacher's instruction, the children all greeted Sheila with "Good morning, Mrs. Chambers."

And then Caleb was at Joan's side, pulling her to the front and center to stand next to Sheila. "This is my Great Grandma Joan," he said proudly. "And you can call her..." He looked up at Joan's face, suddenly looking at a loss for words.

"Mrs. Walker," Joan whispered into his ear.

"Mrs. Walker," he repeated aloud.

"Good morning, Mrs. Walker," the class said. Joan smiled, and an unexpected joy bubbled up from deep within. As a young girl, she'd always admired her teachers and hoped one day to become one herself. But life as a pastor's wife had been full and fulfilling.

Now she was on the brink of an opportunity to share a small role in helping educate this enthusiastic group of second graders. *You are certainly full of surprises,* she whispered in her spirit to God, and a scripture popped into her mind. *Delight yourself in the Lord, and He will give you the desires of your heart.*

Within a few minutes, she found herself sitting with a little girl who barely spoke English. Her parents were migrant workers, and shy little Amelia was struggling to read a language she couldn't even speak fluently. Her large brown eyes locked on Joan's, pleading for help.

With a small stack of sight words and pictures on index cards, Joan set to work helping Amelia on her journey to literacy. Their twenty minutes together passed quickly, but by the end of it she was able to identify more than half of the words without looking at the pictures on the back. "Good job, Amelia," Joan said, giving her a warm smile. "We'll learn the rest next time."

After Amelia, a little boy named Cameron walked up to her with his reader in hand. A note from the teacher, who was leading a reading group at the back of the room, explained the process of partner reading. Joan was to read one page aloud to the boy and then he would read the other page to her. "Give him time to sound out words he doesn't know before you help him," the note said.

So Joan and Cameron sat side-by-side and read a tale about a boy and his dog. "Have you ever had a dog?" she asked the little guy.

He shook his head forlornly.

"Well maybe some day you will," she replied, thinking about Thumper and all the joy that pup had brought her husband and was now bringing her great grandson.

Before she knew it, the hour was up and it was time to leave. Caleb raced over and gave her and Sheila big hugs before he left for recess.

"Thank you so much for your help this morning," Julie Harding said. "The kids love one-on-one attention like that."

Joan nodded. "I think I had as much fun as they did." Sheila agreed.

As they walked out of the school building, Sheila suggested they go out for lunch.

"I wish I could, dear. But I've got plans," Joan replied.

"Really?"

"Yes. I'm having lunch with Margie, my new neighbor. We're thinking about starting a Bible study at Shoreline, so we're going to discuss it today."

"You amaze me, Mom," Sheila said.

"I do?"

"Yes. You remind me of Dad," Sheila replied, her voice filled with emotion as she added, "Always ready to serve."

Joan turned and hugged her, tears filling her eyes. "Now that's just about the sweetest thing anyone's ever said to me," she replied. And in that instant, she realized Phil's words were true. God had a purpose for her life. Even now.

NOTE FROM THE AUTHOR

As the *Sandy Cove* series continues to unfold, God has been teaching me about the many layers of His endless grace. Beginning with Michelle's original quest for truth in *Out of a Dream*, a thread of His divine grace has been woven into the tapestry of the lives of the characters in *Through the Tears, Into Magnolia*, and *Around the Bend*. The same holds true in *From the Heart*.

Starting over is never easy. Whether it is a new home in an unfamiliar area, a change of jobs, or the loss of a loved one, we all experience seasons of disequilibrium, when the world seems tilted and the future uncertain.

As Joan's journey through loss and grief unfolded, I yearned for her to find a new sense of purpose. Something that would fill her heart with hope and give her life new meaning.

Just as He has faithfully done for me in many different seasons of struggle, God came through for Joan. He used her beloved Phil to deliver a message of faith and encouragement at a time when she was about to succumb to despair.

Your situation may be similar or very different from hers. But if you are in your own struggle to find meaning and purpose, or are facing decisions that confuse and overwhelm you or sorrows too hard to bear, I pray that God will speak grace into your life. Just as Joan candidly shared her fears and sorrow with Him, I urge you to do the same.

The sweetest times I've experienced with God flowed out of the most gut-wrenching prayers. When I've let go of all my pretenses of self-control and perceived spirituality and cried out in utter desperation, God has made His presence intimately known; listened patiently to my fears, frustrations, and heartaches; and the lifted me into His ever-loving arms. These are the moments He's spoken Truth into my life, built my faith, and taught me about His boundless grace.

I've learned that nothing is wasted in His economy. For every season of brokenness, there is a hidden treasure of promise— a way He intends to redeem your pain and turn it into a blessing, not only for you, but for others as well.

This is the secret Jesus spoke of when He spoke of giving away your life to find it. (Matthew 10:39) When Joan tried to hold onto her old life, she was empty. At her age, it's understandable that she felt her purpose was over. She'd ministered alongside her pastor husband for many years. But now he was gone, and she was an old woman.

It took Phil's words of love and encouragement to reach down from heaven and remind her of the blessing of service. When she stepped out in faith once again and began to give her life away to the students in Caleb's class, she discovered a new chapter of fulfillment, meaning, and purpose.

The dichotomy of God—give and you will receive. Give of your heart, your time, your life, and you will receive joy and fulfillment in return.

One of my favorite songwriters, Christopher Rice, wrote a song called "Go Light Your World." Just as Joan learned that her joy would be found in giving herself away, the lyrics of this song inspire listeners to carry whatever light God has given them and run into the darkness to find those who need it.

If you are stuck in a place of emptiness or loss, I pray God will lift your eyes to the opportunities He has for you to give yourself away. As Chris Rice exhorted in his song, "Carry your light and run into the darkness." You will be blessed.

As I finish this fifth book in the Sandy Cove series, I'm seeking God's purpose for me as well. Does He have more stories of Michelle's family to share? Time will tell.

In the meantime, please keep in touch. I'd love to hear from you. Drop me an email, and connect with me on Facebook, where I post information about new books, special offers, and general life thoughts. I am so very thankful for you.

In Christ,

Rosemary Hines

rosemary.w.hines@gmail.com
https://www.facebook.com/RosemaryHinesAuthorPage
www.rosemaryhines.com

ACKNOWLEDGMENTS

My heartfelt thanks go to my cover team—Benjamin Hines and Natalie Knudsen, for creating a beautiful cover that communicates the bittersweet story of *From the Heart*. Although the saying goes, "Don't judge a book by its cover," I know this cover will captivate my readers.

Big thanks also go to my dear friend, Joy Frum, whose quaint shed inspired Phil's workshop in both *Around the Bend* and *From the Heart*. It was the perfect setting for this cover, and I'm blessed to be able to share it with my readers.

I'm very grateful for my editor, Nancy Tumbas, and my proofreader, Bonnie Vander Plate. Their tireless attention to detail is essential in the refining and polishing of each of my novels. They encourage, inspire, and assist me as professionals and friends.

The ongoing support of my husband, family, and friends helps me move forward with each story. And my wonderful, gracious readers inspire me with their words of encouragement. When I receive an email from one of them, it makes my day. I have the best readers in the world, and I thank God for each and every one!

BOOKS BY ROSEMARY HINES

Sandy Cove Series Book 1

Out of a Dream

Sandy Cove Series Book 2

Through the Tears

Sandy Cove Series Book 3

Into Magnolia

Sandy Cove Series Book 4

Around the Bend

Sandy Cove Series Book 5

From the Heart

CPSIA information can be obtained at www.ICGtesting.com
Printed in the USA
LVOW11s2007250516

489946LV00001B/88/P

9 781505 249354